The Austrian *schloss* was breathtaking!

''You didn't do it justice when you described it,'' Janet said to Stephen of the mountain hotel, a place that had once been his home. ''It's out of a fairy tale!''

He laughed at her enthusiasm. ''You're a romantic,'' he said, ''and I don't suppose you'll ever be cured.''

''I don't want to be,'' she told him simply. ''It must be awful to see everything in a dim, gray light.''

''The *schloss* is often dim and gray.'' His face was suddenly grim. ''When the wind and snow are blowing, it's easy to imagine it as Dracula's castle . . . and sometimes I've been known to prefer it that way.''

Janet shivered, and not just from the cold mountain air.

Jean S. MacLeod, the author of more than fifty romance novels, lives with her husband on an isolated peninsula in Scotland's Western Highlands. From her doorstep she has a breathtaking view of the Hebrides. "In these surroundings," she says, "it must surely be possible to go on writing for a very long time." Indeed, her ideas and words are as fresh and romantic as ever.

Books by Jean S. MacLeod

HARLEQUIN ROMANCE

1613—MOMENT OF DECISION
1693—ADAM'S DAUGHTER
1719—THE RAINBOW DAYS
1845—TIME SUSPENDED
2024—JOURNEY INTO SPRING
2142—ISLAND STRANGER
2191—SEARCH FOR YESTERDAY
2366—BRIEF ENCHANTMENT
2414—BLACK SAND, WHITE SAND
2482—MEETING IN MADRID
2747—VALLEY OF THE SNOWS
2837—THE APOLLO MAN

CALL BACK THE PAST

Jean S. MacLeod

Harlequin Books

TORONTO • NEW YORK • LONDON
AMSTERDAM • PARIS • SYDNEY • HAMBURG
STOCKHOLM • ATHENS • TOKYO • MILAN

Original hardcover edition published in 1989
by Mills & Boon Limited

ISBN 0-373-17047-5

Harlequin Romance first edition 1989

Printed in U.S.A.

CHAPTER ONE

FOR the first time since he had taken her to Beeston as an orphan to give her a home, her godfather had asked her to do something for him.

'Find Alice Silton for me, Janet,' he had said, looking up from the legal documents which crowded his desk in the office they had shared in Gray's Inn for the past two years. 'I'm a busy man and I've done my best to trace her without result. I have only two clues to her whereabouts and these haven't got me very far.'

'Alice Silton?' Janet repeated the name with curiosity, her eyes thoughtful. 'The Alice you were once in love with?'

His expression told her that 'once' had been the wrong word to use. He was still in love. Richard Cosgrave had remained a bachelor, building up a successful career as a barrister in London after he had qualified all those years ago, but still retaining Beeston as a family home. With the hope of one day bringing Alice Silton to live there as his wife?

'What happened?' Janet asked, laying aside the brief she had been studying before she sent it to be photocopied in the outer office where she generally worked.

'Nothing dramatic.' Her godfather rose from his desk, crossing to the long window which overlooked the sunny courtyard. 'We went our separate ways. We were both ambitious and I knew too late that she was in love with me.' He stood with his back to her, a tall, distinguished-looking figure in his conventional dark suit, the bright sunlight picking out the few grey hairs silvering his head as he remained silent for a moment, remembering the past. 'We quarrelled over something we should have discussed sensibly. I realised that afterwards when she had gone. It was a bitter parting, Jan, because I threw all sorts of accusations at her in my utter unbelief. "How could you be in love with me and go so far away? How can you talk about love and do this thing to me?" I demanded. She tried to reason with me, saying that Paris wasn't so far away, but I wouldn't listen. To me, it was the end of the world at the time. I had my career to think about and my father was dying. I just had to make good for my mother's sake, and I was only at the beginning of my studies.'

'Did you ask her to wait for you?' asked Janet slowly.

'Not in so many words. I was hurt and disappointed—not able to think straight, I suppose—and she had her own career to consider. She had a wonderful singing voice and she had a chance to make good in Paris, but I wouldn't recognise that. I was the stubborn male demanding allegiance at all costs, and I refused to listen to her reasoning, yet now I can remember every word of what she said. "I have to take my chance, Richard, now, at this moment, because it may never happen again. We both have a long way to go and you may change your mind about me." I think these words were burned into my brain from the moment she uttered them.'

He turned from the window, his back to the revealing light.

'I know now that she had been waiting for my denial, willing me to tell her that I would never change, but I wasn't able to find the right words to answer her because of the bitterness in my heart. I had been rejected and the world was turned upside-down. At twenty-two, words didn't come easily because I expected her to understand how much I needed her without having to tell her. Things are different these days, I suppose,' he added quietly, 'and you would be more sensible, I dare say, but I let two whole months go by without writing to her, and by that time it was too late. She had gone. I didn't ask her to marry me before we parted because I wasn't ready. I had nothing to offer her at the age of twenty-two, no great prospects, no success.'

'Was success what she really wanted?' Janet asked.

'I couldn't be sure. Her voice was outstanding and she wanted to be in opera.'

'Do you know where she is now or if she is still—available?' Richard came to stand beside her, gazing down at his untidy desk. 'You said you had two clues.'

'Yes.' He picked up some papers. 'I've been making enquiries for some time—over a year now—and Alice has been seen in Austria by a mutual friend, first in Salzburg, then in Uttendorf and also in Innsbruck. The other information is that she probably married in Paris and moved on from there.'

'It isn't a lot to go on,' remarked Janet on her way to the door, 'and if she has married——'

'She was widowed soon afterwards. I'm sure about that, otherwise I wouldn't be persisting in my search for her.' He walked beside her to the door while she wondered why he should be telling her all this now after so many years of silence. 'This latest information I have is urgent, Jan,' he added, 'and I can't follow it up because I have to be in New York for two weeks on the Cahill brief. Alice has been seen twice in Salzburg at the opera, and I hoped to go there next week to try to trace her, but now that is impossible when I must be in New York.' He paused to draw breath, looking at her anxiously. 'I would like you to go to Austria instead of me,' he said. 'You have successfully traced a client's relatives several times, and your help now would be invaluable.'

Two sudden dimples appeared at the corners of Janet's

mouth as she suppressed a smile.

'Is this a business assignment?' she asked.

'It's more than that,' he replied. 'I'm asking you to go to Austria because you are nearest to me, someone I can trust implicitly, and because I know you can do it.'

Janet looked out through the window at the bright sunlight gilding the new leaves on the courtyard trees, turning everything to gold against the cloudless April sky.

'You're offering me an unexpected holiday,' she said.

'You deserve it. You've worked hard and constantly all winter, Jan, and it's time you took a break.'

'A working brief!' she laughed.

'You've always wanted to go to Austria, and this is the right time of year to see the Tyrol in all its grandeur. You won't be working all the time, so you will have ample opportunity to enjoy yourself. In fact,' he added with some complacence, 'I think you will enjoy the trip. I'm booked on the Orient Express, and I can easily substitute your name on the ticket.'

'By train?' Janet said. 'I thought you would be flying out.'

'It's been a long-standing ambition of mine to travel on the Express, and Alice has also seen in Innsbruck where you will leave the train and travel on by coach.'

'How long do you expect me to stay there?' Janet asked, already excited by the prospect of travelling by such a romantic route.

'Until you find Alice for me,' he said, opening the door for her. 'I haven't booked a return journey, so you might prefer to fly back to London. Nigel Bannister will take over in our absence,' he added briefly. 'It's time we gave him more responsibility.'

The thought of the romantic journey by the famous train, even though she would be going only half-way to Venice, quickened Janet's heartbeats as she prepared for her unexpected adventure. Flying out to Innsbruck would have been quicker, she realised, but she had been offered this unexpected plus to make her mission a pleasure as well as a task, and she was prepared to enjoy the experience, since her regular holiday in the summer of the previous year had been marred by incessant rain.

She booked her godfather a flight to New York by Concorde, driving him to Heathrow before she returned to Gray's Inn to complete her own arrangements in the afternoon. Before Richard had boarded the famous jet he had handed her a fading snapshot of a young girl in a short white skirt with a tennis racquet in her hand, but that wasn't much to go on after twenty-eight years. The girl in the snapshot looked surprisingly young and somehow vulnerable, her hair cut in the then-fashionable shoulder-length 'bob', the ends curling provocatively against her freckled skin, while her slim ankles were encased in little white socks which added to the illusion of immaturity. Yet Alice Silton had held firm where her own ambitions were concerned, deciding that her career should have its chance when marriage had seemed out of the question between her and Richard for many studious years. The inevitability of their parting might have seemed natural to her, but possibly not the bitterness.

Of course, Janet thought, she might not have loved Richard quite so ardently as he had loved her, putting the thought of marriage behind him ever afterwards. Until now!

A strange quest, she thought, getting ready for her journey, and one which might involve her in a great deal of doubt. Alice could have changed out of all recognition by the time she found her.

If she found her, she was forced to correct herself as the glass door leading to the outer office opened and a small, fair-haired girl looked in.

'There's someone here asking to see Mr Richard,' she

announced. 'I've told him he's away in New York, but he's the sort of person who won't take no for an answer.'

Janet frowned.

'Perhaps he has an interview lined up,' she suggested. 'Have you checked the list of Mr Richard's appointments?'

'He wouldn't give his name, and I don't think he even believed that Mr Richard had gone to America.'

Janet sighed. 'That sort of person! Did he say what he wanted?'

'To see someone connected with the firm. I gathered he wasn't going to settle for a typist, however polite I tried to be!' Deborah laughed.

'Show him in, if you must.' Janet gathered some papers together. 'Where was Nigel?'

'In court. He said he might be late back.'

Glancing at her watch, Janet rose to her feet. This couldn't be important, and she had plenty of other work to do before five o'clock. When she turned from her desk a tall, broad-shouldered man in a grey lounge suit was already at the door, filling up the whole aperture, it seemed, as her eyes were held by his compelling gaze. He was the sort of man who would make his presence felt anywhere, and there was a scarcely concealed glint of impatience in his flint-grey eyes as they looked at each other.

'I had hoped to meet Richard Cosgrave,' he announced, 'but I hear he has gone to America.'

Janet had the distinct impression that he doubted Deborah Dunbar's statement.

'I can assure you that he has gone to New York,' she said with professional calm. 'He left this morning, but if there is anything I can do for you, I'm quite willing to try, Mr——'

She left the suggestion open, feeling that she should at least know his name.

He took a step towards her across the room, and a shaft of sunlight from the window lit up his face where anger and frustration was plain to be seen, and Janet found herself drawing back from it with a feeling of alarm. This man could be dangerous if he was thwarted in his determination to pursue a purpose which was evidently important to him.

'I can't promise you an interview with Mr Cosgrave for at least a month,' she told him with dignity. 'If you can afford to wait that long, I'll take your name and address and give you a date.'

'That won't be necessary,' he said in a low, taut voice. 'I'll call again.'

Deborah came back into the room, holding a blue paper wallet in her hand.

'Your tickets and travelling arrangements for Innsbruck,' she said, laying it on Janet's desk. 'I thought you would like to have them right away.' She glanced at the stranger standing in the middle of the room with renewed interest. 'I know you're very busy,' she added. 'Can I do anything to help?'

'No, thank you, Debbie.' Janet was conscious of their visitor looking at the wallet with its unmistakable Orient Express logo, lying between them on the desk. 'I'll tidy up here and get away early. I leave at eleven o'clock tomorrow morning so I won't be able to get in before then. Nigel will be here, though, and I'm sure you will manage.'

She smiled at the typist, turning back to her unexpected visitor with a brief gesture of dismissal.

'I'm sure you'll understand,' she suggested. 'I have a lot to do before I catch the train to Austria. If you'll excuse me. . .'

He walked past her to the door, following Deborah out, but not before Janet had experienced a decided sense of not being in control of a situation which should have been perfectly straightforward. Whatever he had come for, whatever he wanted, this man would pursue the issue to a conclusion, however long it took to do so.

Dismissing their meeting, she concentrated on her own affairs. There was last-minute packing to be done and some necessary mending before she could strap up her travelling-case, make her supper and, hopefully, sink into bed for a good night's sleep. She wondered how Nigel Bannister would cope while she and Richard were away, deciding that it would give the young trainee much needed experience, and then she wondered, albeit sleepily, what Nigel was doing at that very moment. He had asked her out once or twice, but their conversation hadn't progressed much beyond the case of the moment, and she told herself that she was glad that he hadn't returned to the office before she had left as she hadn't been prepared to cope with court talk before she left on her mission for Richard. Finally, she fell asleep, thinking about Austria.

In the morning she was up early and on her way to Victoria by nine o'clock. Beeston was a forty-minute journey on the Underground to Piccadilly, and she decided to take a taxi from there to Victoria, thinking that this was indeed the start of a wonderful experience, as well as something she could do for Richard after all his love and kindness to her in the past. They had been friends rather than god-daughter and guardian, and it was strange that he had never mentioned Alice Silton to her in any detail before. She took out the snapshot which she had placed in the Orient Express wallet with her tickets, studying Richard's lost love once again in an attempt to discover what Alice had really been like, but the pretty, fading image of the girl in the tennis dress smiled back at her impartially, as if the past had dimmed for her as inevitably as her picture on the badly developed snapshot.

Janet thrust it back into her wallet as the taxi drew up at the station entrance. The heady sense of excitement she had experienced the evening before was still uppermost as she made her way to join the boat train waiting so elegantly for her on the platform. No wonder Richard had made it an ambition, she thought, looking along the immaculate line of brown and cream coaches which would take her on the first part of her journey to the Channel port.

Walking leisurely behind her porter, she had an odd feeling of being watched, but she was quick to dismiss this as a figment of her too-active imagination. Her mission was hardly the stuff of a successful whodunnit, and she even smiled at the ridiculous suggestion. Nevertheless, she was oddly conscious of someone following close behind her, even though most of her fellow-passengers were already aboard the train.

When she drew up at her carriage door she turned abruptly, knocking the newspapers from the hand of a man who had come up behind her. Flint-grey eyes challenged her immediately.

'Oh—I'm sorry!' she began. 'But—we've already met!' she added incredulously. 'You came to my guardian's office yesterday—in Gray's Inn.'

He gathered up his scattered newspapers with a hint of impatience which made her feel suddenly gauche and incompetent, but instead of walking on up the platform he stood waiting, their eyes level at last as she mounted the step to her carriage.

'I have apologised,' she reminded him, 'and you were very close.'

'We have both run things rather fine.' The remembered voice, deep and resonant, still held an edge of impatience. 'It's almost eleven o'clock.'

'And the Express always leaves on time!' She smiled at him. 'This is quite a coincidence, meeting you again.'

He waited for her to turn in the cramped lobby without answering that, and she moved abruptly, angry at what might have been a deliberate snub as he climbed aboard in her wake. Her porter had stored her luggage above the first seat in the coach and she tipped him generously while she watched the man in the grey suit find his own accommodation further down the coach. From where she sat she could just see the tip of his head above one of the newspapers she had knocked from his grasp so carelessly a few minutes ago—the *Financial Times*, no doubt, she speculated drily. It was a coincidence, however, that they should be travelling on the same train, although maybe he was going no further than Paris on business.

The luxurious train moved out exactly at eleven o'clock, speeding swiftly through the countryside she knew so well, the North Downs soon on the horizon and the lovely Kentish countryside happy in its mantle of brilliant green. It was a typical English spring day, the dappled sunlight chased by a brisk little wind across the rolling hills and all the trees in fresh new leaf. The Channel would be blue and calm enough ahead of them and quite soon they would be in France.

A steward made his way between the tables to inform everybody that an early lunch would be served before they reached Folkestone, and she settled down in her comfortable Pullman armchair to relax and read the magazine she had bought at Victoria before she had boarded the train. But the articles she skimmed through failed to hold her interest for very long, as she realised how conscious she was of the man seated at the far end of the coach. Why should he impose his personality upon her like this, she wondered angrily, when they were not even acquainted? Soon, however, she found herself wondering why he had come to seek out her godparent in Gray's Inn and why he had brushed aside her suggestion that she should take his name and make a reservation for him to see Richard at a later date. He had been almost brusque in his refusal, she remembered, trying to dismiss him completely, but during the light meal which followed she felt her eyes drawn to the far end of the coach where he was studying her without reserve. Again and again their eyes met confusingly until she was forced to look away.

As the train approached Folkestone he rose from his seat, coming to stand beside her table where she was finishing her second cup of coffee.

'I have an apology to make,' he declared, the flint-grey eyes steady on her own. 'I should have acknowledged you when we literally bumped into each other at Victoria.'

'And I shouldn't have turned round so quickly!' She smiled up at him. 'As a matter of fact, I had a strong feeling of someone following me, which of course was ridiculous!'

Her confession etched a sudden, dark frown between his brows and his eyes were no longer smiling down at her.

'I wouldn't have thought you were so impressionable,' he said briefly. 'Have a pleasant journey!'

He hadn't made any reference to her destination, although he already knew that because Debbie had announced it so unceremoniously when she had brought the Orient Express wallet into the office and laid it on the desk where he could not have failed to see it, so it was really quite a coincidence, after all, travelling on the same train like this. He was the sort of man she would have expected to go by air, because time would mean a lot to him if he was travelling on business, and no doubt she would not see him again if his destination was Paris.

During the Channel crossing, although the Orient Express passengers occupied a small saloon with a private bar, he was conspicuous by his absence, preferring to pace the decks, no doubt, rather than remain below in the overheated atmosphere of the saloon. When she considered the idea of going up for a breath of fresh air she rejected it, not wanting to meet him face to face in case those all-seeing grey eyes might accuse her of following him in her turn.

She did not see him again until she walked off the ferry at

Boulogne and crossed the rails to the long line of opulent blue and gold *wagons-lits* waiting on the platform on the other side, each carriage identified by name. For a moment she hesitated, wondering which way to turn in order to find the name on her ticket.

'Having trouble?' The voice was quite familiar now, the guarded smile only to be expected.

'My porter's miles ahead of me,' she confessed. 'I suppose I was guilty of daydreaming a little as we came off the ferry.'

'Let me help you,' he suggested, taking her ticket wallet from her to walk slightly ahead to where her missing porter was waiting with her luggage together with her cabin steward.

'You're new to all this,' he remarked, his manner touching her on the raw for some reason which she could not quite explain.

'No,' she answered swiftly and a trifle defiantly. 'I'm quite used to travelling abroad on business.'

But always with Richard, she remembered, suddenly feeling very much alone and strangely vulnerable.

'You'll soon get into the way of things,' he assured her. 'We dine before Paris and you will have a chance to stretch your legs at the Gare de L'Est.'

'You're on your way to Paris?' she suggested, conscious of the slightest pause before he answered her.

'No,' he said. 'I'm going on.'

'To Innsbruck?' She supposed she was being far too inquisitive. 'Or perhaps you are going all the way to Venice.'

'To Innsbruck,' he agreed, stepping aside to let her follow her steward down the train.

Her cabin seemed a long way back, but soon her steward was unlocking a door in the polished wood panelling and she was ushered into the neat little cabin where she would spend a part of her journey crossing Europe to the Austrian border, and the sense of excitement and adventure claimed her again as she unpacked her night attire and washed quickly to refresh herself.

Taking out the snapshot of Alice Silton to study it once more, she wondered about her godfather's lost love. Alice would now be in her late forties, and in all probability was still married to the man who had taken his place in her affections all those years ago. But why had she left France and gone to Austria, as Richard's second clue seemed to suggest? Could she have been widowed in Paris? Why, then, had she stayed in France, or wherever, instead of returning to England to find Richard again? Perhaps people didn't do that sort of thing in these days, she reasoned, although it would have been the sensible thing to do. And why hadn't she written? Not once in all these years, Richard had said.

She put the snapshot back into the wallet, looking out through her window, but the flat countryside between the Channel and Paris failed to hold her attention as her thoughts led her down into the past. Soon her steward came to announce that dinner would be served in half an hour, and she slipped into the short-skirted dinner dress she had packed for the occasion and made her way along the swaying corridor to the bar-salon where many of her fellow-travellers were already gathered. The salon was crowded and she flattened herself against the wall to look about her for a moment before she finally ordered a pre-dinner drink. A baby grand piano took up much of the space ahead of her, with a lively young pianist obliging with nostalgic requests for the tunes of yesterday, the songs and ditties of a more elegant age when the famous train had first been built.

Smiling, she listened until one of the salon tables was vacated and she was able to sit down as a white-coated steward came to take her order.

'André will mix you a Bellini or a martini with equal skill,' a voice assured her casually. 'I can recommend them.'

The flint-eyed stranger sat down beside her.

'I ought to know your name,' she suggested,' if we're to keep meeting like this.'

'Mine is Stephen Kempson,' he said without hesitation. 'And yours?'

'I'm Janet Blair,' she told him. 'I work for my godfather and we're very close because he brought me up. I suppose I look at him as a sort of father-figure I've always needed.'

For a moment she thought that he was no longer interested in what she had to say as his gaze followed hers down the luxurious coach to the tiny bar at its far end, where the pianist was picking out the notes of 'When I Grow Too Old to Dream', a song he was far too young to remember.

'I wondered about that.' He paid for both drinks as the steward placed them on the table before them. 'I wondered why you were travelling to Austria without the usual paraphernalia of skis and rucksacks which generally clutter up the corridors even at this time of year. There's still enough snow on the higher reaches of the Tyrol to justify the late enthusiasts on the mountains.'

'Isn't it dangerous to ski so late in the season?' she asked, sipping the smooth concocotion in her glass with evident appreciation.

'It depends on one's taste for danger.' He considered her obliquely. 'It can be found anywhere and in different forms. How long have you been working for your godfather?'

The direct question was completely unexpected, and Janet put down her glass before she answered it.

'For three years. I trained as a secretary and then Richard suggested I should work for him in Gray's Inn. I took extra tuition and got to know about briefs and that sort of thing. The court work is completely absorbing, as you can imagine, and I love every minute of it.'

'What else do you do?' His tone was abrupt.

'Now that we have Debbie as a general dogsbody in the office, I do a lot of the follow-up work on contracts and that sort of thing. I also cope with references and unravel complications when time is of the essence.'

'I see.' He put down his empty glass. 'How was the Bellini?' he asked.

'Very smooth. I haven't tasted one before. Is it a speciality of the train?'

'Second only to champagne! Will you have another?'

'Thank you, no. I think I'd like to wait till I can have some wine with my dinner.'

The crowd round the piano was thinning; other diners were making their way towards the continental dining-cars ahead of them.

'You had better join me,' Stephen Kempson suggested. 'Single seats are hard to come by, but we could easily manage two. It's one sitting before Paris.'

He stood aside, and suddenly her heart was beating madly under the fine lace of her bodice as she preceded him along the train. She could call this adventure if she liked, but it was also much needed companionship, because she had never liked travelling on her own. It didn't matter if Stephen Kempson thought her naïve or foolishly uncomplicated compared with the women he usually met. All she needed was the subtle sense of warmth which now enfolded her as they sought a table for two in one of the dining-cars ahead of them.

The first car was fully occupied, the diners already being served, but he strode forward with the confidence she expected of him and soon they were seated facing each other at a table for two.

'It makes it easier to talk,' he observed, 'instead of having to listen to the general conversation at a table for four.'

Janet was looking about her, entirely enthralled by the gleaming brass and silver and the Lalique glass panels between the wide observation windows beyond which the flat countryside of northern France was flashing past. Dusk was gathering and an aureate glow hovered in the west making a band of light along the horizon and filling the coach with a subtle warmth which sank deeply into her heart. The little pink-shaded lamps adorning each table, and the orchids in their silver containers, added to the magic so that she felt she could go on sitting there for the rest of her life.

Stephen handed her the menu in which she lost herself for a moment.

'There's so much to choose from,' she decided at last. 'What would you recommend?'

'I hardly know your taste,' he pointed out. 'Remember, we have just met.'

'We met yesterday,' she mused, 'which seems an age ago.'

'Yes.' He studied her closely before he turned his full attention to the menu.

'How do you feel about caviare?' he asked.

'I don't like it. That's probably a terrible admission,' she smiled, 'but I have tried it—once.'

'Since once was apparently enough,' he said, 'I'll suggest *saumon fumé d'Ecosse et sa Brunois*—smoked Scottish salmon to us English!'

'You speak French very well!'

'I was born in France and I work here.'

'But you are typically English.'

'Hence the *saumon fumé d'Ecosse!*'

'How long have you worked in France?'

'Most of my adult life, although I was educated in England.'

The steward came to take their order and Janet found herself relaxing completely. Stephen Kempson was the perfect companion, choosing the wine they would drink with their braised duckling and afterwards the fine cheeses and fresh fruit salad with sherbet which completed their meal.

The lights of Paris were filling the skyline as they drank their coffee, and soon they were pulling up at the Gare de L'Est where he had suggested that she might like to stretch her legs.

'You'll have had enough of the train by the time we reach Innsbruck,' he suggested.

'I've never slept on a train before,' she confessed. 'It's all new and very exciting as far as I'm concerned. I've flown to Milan and several times to New York, but that was always on business.'

'While this journey is solely for pleasure?' He turned to observe her with the penetrating look in his eyes she was beginning to expect, and she found herself flushing under his scrutiny.

'Not entirely,' she was bound to say, 'but my mission is rather personal. It has nothing to do with business in the ordinary way—it has to do with tracing someone my godfather knew many years ago.' He remained silent and she rushed on, 'I have to do this because I feel that I owe him so much and I have time at my disposal. I can stay in Austria for three or four weeks, and then it *will* be something of a holiday.' She smiled up at him. 'If I haven't any success in Salzburg I shall go on searching elsewhere.'

'Do I ask what happens after Salzburg?' he queried. 'Or am I in line for a snub?'

'Quite honestly,' she told him, 'I don't know. I have an address in Salzburg where I might pick up another thread, but after that—who knows?'

He got to his feet, unsmiling now as he stood aside for her to precede him along the coach, and some of the warmth she had felt during their shared meal evaporated. At the coach door, however, he turned to help her down the steep steps on to the platform, reaching up towards her, and suddenly their eyes were level. In his she could read a faint doubt, a puzzlement he evidently could not hide, and then his strong hands were supporting her and she was jumping down on to the platform beside him with all doubts swiftly dispelled.

They walked under the lights the full length of the train and on into comparative darkness where they stood contemplating the silhouette of Paris in the enchanted dusk. Ringed by lights, the city seemed to glow, the dome of the Sacré-Coeur omnipotent on its commanding hill, the avenues dark under their guardian planes until they merged in another blaze of light at junctions or marched beside the sombre water of the Seine.

'I'm glad we came out,' Janet said. 'You have to feel part of the night to appreciate its beauty. I believe I can even see a star over there making a first appearance in the sky.'

'You'll appreciate the Tyrol,' he decided, turning back towards the train. 'It bears no resemblance to Paris, yet it has the same sort of magic. You're lucky to be seeing it for the first time.'

He helped her back on to the train, but this time his touch was light and impersonal, as if she had accepted assistance from one of the willing cabin stewards who stood there ready to help.

Walking ahead of him along the coaches, she wondered if this was to be the end of their acquaintance, but he stopped at the entrance to the bar-salon, searching for a table in a corner where he ordered champagne.

'It's going to be too dark to look out of the window,' he said, 'and far too early to go to bed. Believe it or not, people dance in here, and if your cabin's anywhere near you're going to hear the noise anyway, so you may as well relax for an hour and listen to the music.'

'I'd thought of an early night,' she confessed, 'but you've convinced me that I'll be missing quite a lot and not doing very much about my beauty sleep! I can't see how anyone can possibly dance, though; there's so little room between the tables.'

'Where there's a will!' he quipped, checking the champagne as the steward presented the bottle. 'Perhaps we ought to try.'

They danced several times to the nostalgic tunes of the twenties and thirties hammered out on the piano at the far end of the salon, laughing when the swaying train thrust them close and collapsing into their respective seats when the music stopped. Towards midnight he ordered tea, which was accompanied by delicious little cakes on a silver dish.

'Perhaps sandwiches would have been more to your liking,' he suggested, but Janet shook her head.

'I've never tasted such cakes!' she declared, her eyes glowing in the soft lamp-light. 'You certainly know the right thing to do.'

His mouth hardened a little.

'The vibrant atmosphere of a bar-salon isn't exactly my idea of perfection,' he returned drily.

'No,' Janet heard herself saying. 'I think you're the out-of-doors type, although I could be wrong because of Paris.'

He laughed.

'I have to work in Paris, but I get away as often as possible, preferably to the mountains.'

'Hence Innsbruck?'

He hesitated.

'Innsbruck or Salzburg—it doesn't really matter.' He poured more champagne into her glass. 'I spent most of my school holidays skiing around Kitzbühel, but recently I haven't been able to get there. Not for any length of time.'

She waited for him to continue, but evidently that was

to be the full extent of his confidences. The salon was emptying as, one by one or in tired couples, their fellow-travellers repaired to their cabins, and Janet glanced at her watch.

'It's past midnight!' she observed, surprised by the way time had flown. 'I had no idea.'

He rose immediately.

'You must want to stay,' she said. 'There are still plenty of dancing partners for you to choose from.'

'I'll take you as far as your cabin,' he said.

Walking ahead of him along the train corridor, she thought how wonderful the evening had been. It had all been very romantic and appealing, although more than once she had been conscious of being studied carefully by her companion. When they had danced she had felt her heart-beats quicken, but, of course, it was all just a fairy-tale because they were no more than ships passing in the night.

They reached her cabin door and she fumbled in her evening bag for her key, sware of his sudden closeness in the narrow corridor as he waited for her to open the door.

'Let me help you,' he suggested, taking the key from her. 'They're not too easy to open.'

Their fingers touched and something almost electric passed between them, an attraction such as she had never experienced before, but instantly she pulled away.

'I think I can manage, thank you!'

He laughed.

'Don't worry,' he said. 'I don't expect to be asked in.'

Janet drew in a swift breath.

'Thank you for tonight,' she said stiffly. 'It was all very kind of you.'

He turned on his heel, going away along the corridor before she had opened the door.

In the morning it was light early and she felt an almost irresistible desire to run along the corridor to the salon where they had sat under the silk-shaded wall-lights sipping their drinks the evening before, but she had yet to pack, and breakfast would be served in her cabin. No doubt the bar-salon would be cold and empty.

When the steward brought in her breakfast tray there was a pink carnation lying on her plate with a folded piece of paper beside it. She read it hastily.

'See you at Innsbruck!' Stephen Kempson had written.

Her spirits soared, although she could also tell herself how foolish she was, making far too much of a casual meeting on an international train.

Packing and eating her breakfast at the same time, she was conscious of an excitement which had nothing to do with travelling to strange places, a new feeling which went beyond enchantment to leave her in an odd limbo of delight.

With an hour to spare when her case was finally locked, she walked along the corridor to the salon. It was empty, but she settled down to look out through the wide observation windows at the breathtaking change which the night journey had brought to the scenery. They were in the Vorarlberg with alps on either side and deep gorges plunging down to ice-fed rivers rushing in white majesty to the valley below. Little towns flashed by, their church spires reaching for the sky—St Anton and Landeck and Imst with their rooftops glistening in the morning sun, and snow still on the mountains behind them. Fascinated, she watched the progress of the red engine pulling them up the gradients ahead, the first coaches of the train clearly visible from where she sat as they wound ever upwards in the snow. Above them peak after peak towered in a cloudless azure sky while the tall pines stood motionless between them.

'Makes you think about silence,' her companion of the evening before remarked. She hadn't heard him coming into the salon, her back turned.

'It must be wonderful to climb out there, to walk in the stillness,' she responded, looking round from the window to smile at him. 'But you must have done plenty of that.'

'In my time,' he agreed. 'The mountain air is more to my liking than Paris.'

'It's a pity we can't do what we want more often,' she mused. 'Thank you for the carnation.'

He looked down at her with an amused smile.

'The steward was passing with your tray when they were clearing away the flowers,' he said, 'and I couldn't resist it! I took the opportunity to wish you a pleasant journey. Have you decided what you are going to do after Innsbruck? Surely your real destination is Salzburg?'

The grey eyes challenged hers, questioning her indecision of the evening before.

'I thought about that this morning over my pampered breakfast tray,' she acknowledged, 'and I've decided to go on.'

'You'll enjoy the drive through the Tyrol if you're going by coach,' he said.

'I'd like to go by road,' she told him, 'because I'll see more of the countryside that way. I've loved the train,' she hastened to add, 'but I've found it restricting in some ways. I suppose I can travel to Salzburg by bus.'

He hesitated for no more than a second.

'I intend to hire a car at Innsbruck,' he said. 'If you are in no great hurry, I could take you to Salzburg by road.'

'Oh—that would be lovely!' She had yielded to impulse. 'But, on second thoughts, I could be holding you up,' she concluded.

'I have plenty of time to spare,' he assured her. 'My first appointment in Salzburg isn't till tomorrow.'

'Which means you will even have time for Mozart,' she laughed. 'Are you musically inclined?'

'Not too much. How about you?'

'I can listen with appreciation although not with a great deal of knowledge,' she confessed. 'Richard—my godfather—is the expert.'

'Ah, Richard!' he replied. 'I remember you said how close you were. He evidently trusts your judgement in other things when he sends you so far afield on a mission of great importance to him.'

'He would have come himself if it hadn't been for New York. Something he hadn't expected cropped up at the last moment after he had booked on the train, and so—I had to come instead. It has all been very exciting for me, but as soon as I get to Salzburg I must start to work.'

A steward came past, offering them a lunch menu apiece, and he studied his in silence for a moment.

'Salzburg will enchant you in many ways,' he said at last, 'quite apart from Mozart. It's a city you have to visit again and again to appreciate it properly.'

'You sound as if you know it very well,' she said.

'Every corner of it,' he admitted. 'Even nature looks favourably on Salzburg, and if you care about history it stands there much the same as it was when the prince-archbishops built a fortress and a cathedral there at the intersection of age-old trade routes. Today it walks hand in hand with a modernity which can never change it. Besides all that,' he added less serously, 'you will have ample opportunity to indulge your desire for walking in the stillness. There are woods and mountain lakes everywhere, and cable railways to take you there when you are too tired or too lazy to walk.'

'I would need much longer than three weeks to see it all,' Janet decided, 'and I have—other things to do.'

'Yes.' He went back to studying his menu. 'Have you decided what you want to eat?'

'Something light after the efforts of last night!' she

decided. 'Omelette, I think.' She put her menu aside. 'But don't let that influence you if you would like a substantial meal.'

'An omelette will be fine,' he agreed. 'I'll cope with a heavier meal this evening. Have you any idea where to stay in Salzburg?'

'Richard suggested the Goldener Hirsch, but I thought there might be time enough to book in there once I had reached Innsbruck.'

He looked slightly surprised at her choice of hotels, but that was all.

'We'd better make sure of a table,' he said, 'before the rush begins.'

While they ate she thought about his background—the little he had told her—what he did for a living. Something professional, she supposed, looking at the strong, well-manicured hands while he manipulated his knife and fork, yet the suggestion of an out-of-doors life was very strong and he had already admitted his love of the mountains.

Well, no doubt she would never know unless she was prepared to ask even more personal questions which he might easily resent. Far better to think of it all as an adventure, the kind that might stay in her memory for a long time, but one which he would probably forget as soon as they parted company in Salzburg. She had sketched in most of her own background for him, including the fact that she was very fond of Richard and that she was prepared to do anything for her godfather because he had done so much for her.

What matter? They were no more than casual acquaintances, fellow-travellers who would go their separate ways in the end, ships passing in the night.

His cabin was somewhere at the back of the train and she did not see him again until she was collecting her luggage on the platform at Innsbruck. Perhaps even now, she thought, she should complete the journey to Salzburg by bus

Across the busy square she could see the line of buses waiting, but she made no movement towards them.

'I won't be more than a few minutes,' Stephen Kempson told her as he came towards her 'The hire office is just across the way.'

She watched the stream of their fellow-travellers hailing taxis or being met by couriers or staff from the hotels, wondering if she would have been wiser to have taken the bus for Salzburg which was already pulling out. After all, she didn't know this man.

'All set?'

He got out of a big, powerful Mercedes-Benz which had drawn up at the pavement where she stood, putting her luggage into the boot before he held open the passenger door for her to get in. It had started to rain, a thin drizzle that would surely clear before long.

'Pity we can't have the roof open for the first part of the journey,' he apologised as he re-started the engine, 'but the rain will clear before Salzburg.'

In spite of the drizzle, the journey along the level valley of the Inn was truly spectacular as alp after alp came into view, glittering against the skyline on either side of the broad green river as it wound its way to join the blue Danube.

'I couldn't have imagined this!' Janet exclaimed. 'Somehow, I thought all the snow would have gone.'

'It's green enough on the low ground, but right into the summer months there's snow on the peaks. It's a pity about the mist, but at least you will be able to see the mountains in all their moods.'

She had to acknowledge him as the perfect companion. It was an interlude in her mission which she had not expected and she was determined to make the most of it. At Salzburg they would part with no regrets and that was the way it should be.

'This is a plus!' she declared, settling back in the seat beside him. 'It's so much nicer to have a competent guide to a strange country.'

He smiled at her description.

'I'll do my best,' he promised. 'Just ahead of us are the Kitzbühler Alps. If you look to the right you will see the valley going up among the mountains, unless the mist is too low.'

Behind them the sun had come out, chasing the rain clouds away to reveal the whole panorama of alps on the far side of the valley, and she could only gasp at their magnificence.

'This must be like coming home as far as you are concerned,' she suggested when he slowed down to point out the beauty of the Kitzbühler valley still with a veil of mist hovering over it.

'I spent a lot of time up there before I went to work in Paris,' he told her, driving on. 'We skied a lot in those days, up over the Pass to Mittersill and Zell-am-See. There's a lake up there that seems to mirror the whole world, or so I used to think, with the Saalach far below it and the Watzmann straight ahead. I miss those days,' he admitted, 'because I don't come here as often as I should. It's a long way to travel from Paris for a weekend.'

'You're here now,' she pointed out, 'but surely too late in the season to ski?'

'I have other business in Salzburg,' he said, driving on, and once again she saw the frown darken his face as his handsome mouth firmed into a determined line.

When they reached the border check-point into Bavaria he produced his passport, holding out his hand for hers.

'It's very much a formality,' he said, 'but we have to show them and get them stamped.'

Janet searched in her handbag to produce the necessary document, remembering that she had put it into the Orient Express wallet when it had been returned to her on the train. When she passed it to him, she glanced at him.

'You keep your British passport, I see,' she commented while they waited to drive up to the check-point.

He looked at her sideways.

'I thought you might have discovered how British I am by now,' he said slowly. 'My mother married my father in Paris, where he also worked, and I was registered as a British citizen, although she married again after his death. My stepfather was Austrian.'

'Does your mother live in Austria?' she asked as they moved up the line of vehicles to the check-point.

'Yes.' His reply seemed deliberately non-committal and she supposed she was prying once more as his dark brows came together in a quick frown.

'I'm being inquisitive,' she hastened to admit. 'I shouldn't be asking so many personal questions.'

He chose not to contradict her as he handed over the two passports, but as he did so a small piece of cardboard fell from one of them, landing at the barrier where one of the guards picked it up. Stephen took it, looking down at the snapshot of the girl in the white tennis dress which was all Richard now possessed of his former love.

'This must be yours,' he said. 'It fell from your passport when I handed it over.'

His voice had been like ice, and she could not understand why he should sound so cold.

'I had no idea it was in there,' she said, 'but I'm so glad I didn't lose it. It means so much to Richard, you see, and I shall need it in Salzburg.'

He put his own passport back into his pocket, watching as she returned the faded picture of Alice Silton to the wallet before she put it into her handbag.

It seemed no time after that until they had reached the outskirts of Salzburg, having crossed back into Austria again, and were driving in hazy sunshine into the heart of the city.

'You'll be comfortable enough at the Goldener Hirsch,' he told her, 'and I can recommend the food.'

When he finally drew up at the hotel she was completely taken by surprise.

'It's palatial!' she exclaimed. 'I must watch my expenses, otherwise Richard will read me the riot act!'

While a porter carried in her luggage, Stephen helped her out of the Mercedes. It was over now, she thought, this incredible adventure, and she would never see him again.

Implusively she asked him to dinner.

'You have been very kind to me,' she assured him, waiting for him to refuse.

'Why not?' he said. 'If only to translate the menu for you!'

The frown had gone and his eyes held amusement, which suggested that their evening together might be fun.

'I ought to brush up my French,' she admitted. 'I haven't used it since my schooldays, except on a menu,' she added provocatively.

'You might prefer to try something Austrian tonight,' he suggested. 'Something I can heartily recommend.'

'I'm sure I shall enjoy it,' she told him, her heart lighter by far as she followed the uniformed porter into the hall. Tomorrow would do for Alice Silton, she decided. This evening would be her own.

From the window of her room she had a magnificent view, and she stood there for a long time looking out into the dusky night where the lights of the city were glittering in small clusters to rival the first of the stars. Spires and domes and pinnacles caught what was left of the natural light, with ghostly alps like great white icicles marching away to the horizon on every side, while high above the ancient baroque city and the river which surrounded it a white fortress stood omnipotent on a hill. A magic city, she thought happily, that would live in her memory for a very long time.

When she had unpacked, she lay in a scented bath in the big, tiled bathroom until it was time to dress and go downstairs in search of her unexpected guest. Strange how she had accepted Stephen Kempson almost without question, she mused, but the help he had offered her would account for that. Her thoughts lingered on the long drive through the Tyrol with its majesty of mountains and the rapport which seemed to be developing between them with every passing minute. Until they had crossed from Austria into Bavaria, she admitted reluctantly. Why had he looked so stern as he handed her passport back at the checkpoint? She remembered the snapshot, but assured herself that there could be nothing abut the incident which could possibly concern him.

Giving her hair a final brush, she went down in the lift to find him waiting for her in the foyer. He had changed into a conventional lounge suit and her heart tightened a little as he came towards her.

'Ready to make up for that early lunch on the train?' he asked, guiding her towards the nearest lounge, where little tables were set for pre-dinner drinks with nuts and olives. 'I must confess I'm as hungry as a hunter!'

'I've booked a table for half-past eight,' she told him. 'Is that all right?'

'Perfect,' he agreed. 'How did you find your room?'

'I feel like a visiting film star!' she laughed. 'Never have I seen such a bath!'

'We go in for baths in Salzburg in all shapes and forms, but mostly the curative kind,' he smiled. 'Seriously, though, they have quite a reputation in this part of the world, and some of the people I know in Paris swear by them, but since you're not here for the cure we must think of other things for you to do. You mustn't miss the Alter Markt in the old town or the Residenzplatz, and the churches are a must.'

'Do you know Getreidegasse?' she asked.

'Very well.' There had been the barest pause before he had answered her. 'Why?' he asked.

'I have to go there. I have been given the address of a small shop, a wrought-iron worker's, off the main thoroughfare. It—could be important to me.'

'Getreidegasse isn't hard to find,' he assured her as a waiter came towards them. 'You'll find every type of craft there if that's what you're looking for.'

She would be looking for Alice Silton, but he couldn't be interested in her search or hearing about Alice again. All that was for tomorrow!

The meal they shared was typically Austrian. Stephen chose it with care, selecting the wines and, finally, the cheeses which he felt sure she would enjoy. He had outlined the city's history for her, giving her a good idea of how to get about and what she ought to see, but he had not offered to take her on an extended tour.

'I have someone to meet tomorrow morning,' he excused himself. 'It is a rendezvous I can't pass up.'

And this was to be their final contact, an intimate dinner *à deux* which, for her, had been the fitting climax to a pleasant adventure. No use wishing that it could go on indefinitely, because he had spoken of another rendezvous, which was the logical conclusion to his visit to Austria.

'Thank you for a delightful meal,' he said when she walked with him through the foyer. 'I hope it won't dent your expense account too badly and Richard won't be too displeased with you!'

She followed him through the doorway and into the

scented night.

'I've enjoyed myself so much,' she confessed. 'Thank you, Stephen, once again. It makes a difference to have a—companion in a strange city, particularly for a first meal in the evening.'

Unexpectedly he stooped to kiss her on both cheeks, a gesture which seemed wholly foreign to him, even though he had been brought up in Paris.

'Goodnight,' he said. 'And thank you, Jan!'

He walked away into the shadowy night and Janet stood where he had left her, feeling that the busy world had suddenly stopped. A cool little breeze crept down from the mountains to ruffle her hair and her eyes were suddenly bleak.

Well, that's it, she decided, and I'm a fool to care. I knew all along that this would be a passing thing.

She went directly to her room, standing at the window for several minutes, making sure that he had really gone. And he had gone without looking back, she thought, wondering why he had seemed almost reluctant to help her in her quest for Richard's youthful love.

CHAPTER TWO

JANET'S own reason for being in Salzburg was her first preoccupation the following morning. There would be no looking back, no wishing that her companion of that romantic journey on a famous train would seek her out in this magic city surrounded by mountains which, even now, was casting its spell over her in another way. Full of guilt, she acknowledged how little time she had given to her quest for Alice Silton, but that could be remedied now, she told herself, taking out the snapshot of Alice and hoping to see some of the older woman's character reflected in the faded features of the girl with the tennis racket.

What she saw was a rather sweet-faced young lady with fair, curling hair and pensive eyes who didn't seem to have a care in the world, yet Alice Silton's mouth was firm, her chin rounded and strong, a girl capable of making her own decisions in life, however difficult they might be. Not a determined person in the ordinary way, but one with firmly fixed ideas which would not be easily reversed. Long ago she had gone her own way, either from ambition or necessity, leaving Richard behind.

Janet put the snapshot back into her handbag, determined to forget Stephen Kempson and get down to work.

The clue she followed up was one of the two Richard had given her, and she set out to find Getreidegasse shortly after nine o'clock. Fascinated by the old town, she walked slowly through the Alter Markt, admiring the ancient residences and wrought-iron balconies and the delightful little roof cafés with people already relaxing in the sun, sipping their morning coffee while the busy world hurried past in the street below.

The Getreidegasse, when she found it, was narrow and fascinating, with little arcaded passages leading from it on either side and ornate signs hanging above it to indicate the nature of the business carried on by the shopkeepers below. A gigantic key suspended from a wrought-iron frame was only one of many, and it was a wrought-iron worker's premises she sought. Eventually she found the small shop in an alleyway off the main street. It seemed to be a very old-established business, the entrance low and narrow, but inside was an Aladdin's cave of beautiful workmanship—inn signs, lamps, intricate basketwork and ornaments—all individual pieces worthy of more than a second look.

An old man came through from the back premises, stooping and peering through metal-framed spectacles at her while he waited for her to speak.

'I'm looking for Hans Dietrich,' she explained. 'I believe he works here—or did work here.'

'I am he,' he answered in broken English. 'Can I be of assistance to you?'

Janet produced the faded shapshot, passing it over a counter cluttered with merchandise, and for a moment she thought that he looked startled, but he shook his head as he made an almost instant decision.

'No,' he said. 'I do not recognise this lady.'

Disappointed, Janet turned to go. The picture of Alice she had shown him was not at all clear and he could easily have been mistaken. Before she had reached the doorway he had called her back.

'My brother, Sebastian, will be here soon,' he said. 'He will know. He sees better than I do. I am nearly blind.'

'How soon will your brother return?' she asked.

He considered her question carefully.

'One hour, perhaps. He has gone no further than the Rathaus to order some material.'

Janet went out to roam the narrow streets and alleyways for

an hour until she heard the two-hundred-and-fifty-year-old Glockenspiel carillon ringing out above the ancient rooftops. It was eleven o'clock, and time to go back to the alleyway where the Dietrich brothers had their shop.

Sebastian Dietrich was younger than his brother, and seemed to see a resemblance in the snapshot to someone he knew.

'She came here many years ago,' he remembered, 'when she was a young lady living in Paris, and then we did not see her again for a very long time.' His English was excellent. 'Then she came once more to buy for her employer, she said, ordering replacements for old locks and several fire-baskets which she took away with her as soon as they were ready.'

Eagerly Janet suggested a name.

'Was it Miss Silton—Miss Alice Silton?'

He shook his head.

'No, it was not that. It was another English name.'

Janet hesitated.

'Would it be wrong of me to ask the name of her employer?' she suggested.

'I'm sorry,' he apologised, 'I can't help you further.'

Disappointed for a second time, Janet turned away as the iron bell above the door jangled to announce another customer. When she turned around she came face to face with Stephen Kempson.

'Stephen!' she exclaimed. 'What are you doing here?'

'Shopping,' he answered smoothly. 'Much the same as you.'

'I didn't come to buy anything,' she confessed. 'I was seeking information.'

'Ah!' he said, looking across the counter at Sebastian. 'And were you successful?'

'Not really.' She moved towards the door where Hans was waiting to show her out. 'I must try elsewhere.'

Before the door closed behind her she realised that he was known to the brothers. He was talking swiftly in German to

Sebastian, whose face was now wreathed in welcoming smiles, and suddenly she felt exasperated.

Out in the passageway she stood for a moment, not quite sure which way to turn, and before she had made up her mind the glass door behind her opened and Stephen came out.

'It must have been disappointing for you to have drawn a blank,' he suggested, walking beside her. 'Where do you intend to try now?'

'I don't know.' She was still uncertain what to do. 'It's disconcerting because I don't think they were telling me the truth. Not the whole truth, anyway,' she added.

He walked with her to the junction with Getreidegasse before he asked, 'How important is all this to you?'

'It's very important.' She paused to look at him. 'Stephen, I must find Alice Silton because that's why I am here and because I am working for someone I'm fond of. Richard wants to trace Alice and I mean to do all I can to find her. So far I haven't been very diligent in my efforts because Salzburg has taken my mind off my true reason for being here—Salzburg and its many distractions,' she added deliberately. 'I'm wasting precious time pandering to my own desires.'

'Salzburg is full of distractions,' he agreed, 'but I won't try to wean you away from your quest again, since it means so much to you.'

She tried to apologise.

'I didn't mean you, Stephen. Please believe me when I say I'm sorry. I appreciate your many kindnesses and I'm truly grateful.'

'Grateful enough to share a meal with me?' he asked.

'Of course!'

They turned into the Getreidegasse, walking on the sunny side of the street.

'I have to make an appearance at the Kongresshaus,' he intimated, 'but I should be free by one o'clock. Will you go back to the Goldener Hirsch and I'll pick you up there?'

'I'll walk back,' she decided, 'and look at the shops on the way.'

'Don't walk too far and don't get lost,' he cautioned.

'If I do, I can take a cab!'

'I'll collect you at half-past one,' he offered, smiling as he walked off along the narrow street.

Janet made her way back to the hotel, giving herself time to wash and change before she went down to the foyer to wait for him. Of course, she should have been thinking about Alice Silton, but one afternoon wasn't going to make a great deal of difference to her search for Richard's lost love. She would return to the Dietrichs' shop the following morning to ask more questions, she decided, hoping to break down the odd wall of reserve which Sebastian seemed to have erected between them. She could also ask Stephen about the two brothers, since he seemed to be on friendly terms with them.

Thus justified, she prepared to enjoy the remainder of the day in his company.

Stephen drew up to the hotel in the car he had hired at Innsbruck.

'Ready?' he asked, admiring her with candid eyes. 'I thought we might go out of town where I could show you a mountain trail. You wanted to walk in the stillness,' he reminded her.

She laughed.

'Do you always think of everything?' she demanded. 'I suppose I made that remark on the train.'

'You did.' He handed her into the car. 'We'll cross the bridge and go south, I think,' he decided. 'Then you can see the old city as it was originally and more or less as it still is. We can eat at Schloss Mirabel, if you like, and go on from there.'

It seemed to Janet that all Salzburg was a mass of churches, archbishops' palaces and spectacular towers where the sun sparkled on ancient rooftops, warming the red tiles and glinting across paved squares over which many feet had trodden through the centuries. Enthralled by the views that Stephen presented to her, she was almost reluctant to eat, but eventually he pulled up at a tiny restaurant where tables were set out on a sunny terrace which fronted it among a wealth of trees.

'This will be much quieter than the Schloss,' he remarked, 'and I can also recommend it.'

They ate looking across the river to the imposing fortress standing high above the odd town with a crown of alps surrounding it and the sun picking out the green mountain trails on either side, and afterwards they left the car behind and climbed to the Capucin church and monastery where all the peace of the world seemed to sleep.

'I'll never forget this,' Janet declared, resting her arms on the sun-warmed stone of the wall. 'I'm playing traunt, I know, but it has been well worth it!'

'And time for the mountain trail?' he asked.

'Why not?' she said, smiling up at him. 'I've made up my mind to enjoy my day!'

When they had walked for an hour along winding, wooded pathways where the trees arched above their heads to make a green canopy of shade, they emerged once again on to a high plateau, giving them yet another view of the river and the city itself.

'Stephen,' Janet asked impulsively, 'how well do you know the Dietrich brothers?'

He sat down on an outcrop of rock to consider her question.

'Reasonably well,' he acknowledged. 'Why?'

She sensed some of the same reserve in him that she had found in Sebastian.

'Because they are almost the only contact I have with Alice Silton,' she explained. 'Sebastian admitted that he knew Alice, that she had come to their shop on more than one occasion, but he didn't know her as Alice Silton. He said she had another name, another English name, when they first met, and that she had gone to the shop many years later to buy for an employer. That was all he would say, and he wouldn't tell me the employer's name.'

He looked down at his clasped hands for a moment.

'You could hardly expect him to betray a trust,' he pointed out almost harshly. 'Business people don't talk about their customers to strangers.'

'I know that,' she agreed, 'but I have a feeling there was something else, some other reason for him to refuse me.'

'I can't think of one,' he returned stiffly. 'Unless he felt that you were being intrusive for an ulterior motive of your own.'

'I suppose I was,' she was forced to admit. 'I suppose I had no right to insist.'

'Yet you intend to return?'

'If it would do any good. What would you do?'

He laughed.

'That is hardly the point,' he said. 'I am not searching for Miss Alice Silton.'

'I wonder what the other name was—the other English name,' she mused. 'It could have been Alice's married name. Yes, surely that was it, so why wouldn't he tell me?'

'Because he thought you were too inquisitive.' His tone was light, but still guarded. 'I thought we were going to forget about your mission for half a day?' he reminded her. 'You can go on searching tomorrow.'

As the sun set behind the alps across the Saalach, turning them rose-red against an azure sky, Janet acknowledged a magic she could no longer resist. Stephen Kempson had made this day for her, even though it had been stolen from her allegiance to Richard.

They returned to Salzburg to 'go on the town' as Stephen put it, wandering through the narrow streets to admire the fountains and the lovely old baroque buildings which surrounded every open square, until hunger drove them to a wine tavern in a vaulted medieval cellar where there was folk-dancing on an elevated floor and the food was remarkably good. The bottle of wine he ordered was rich and mellow, relaxing her completely.

'I had no idea Salzburg would be like this,' she confessed. 'I could spend months here and still not feel satisfied.'

'Tomorrow you must take an open cab and see the rest of the city,' he advised. 'You'll find one on the Residenzplat beside the colonnades. They are a must because the horses don't hurry. In fact they are the only way to see old Salzburg. I'm sorry I won't be able to go with you,' he added as he paid his bill and they rose to go because it was almost midnight. 'I have another appointment which I can't postpone.'

'And I must go back to Getreidegasse,' she decided. 'I must speak to Sebastian Dietrich again.'

'It won't get you anywhere,' he predicted, tight-lipped. 'Sebastian is very loyal.'

'To old friends, do you mean?'

'Even to old customers.' He led the way between the tables towards the stone stairway which went up to the entrance and the still busy street above. 'The average Austrian knows how to keep his mouth shut when necessary, and Sebastian is above average.'

Her mouth hardened into a determined line.

'All the same,' she decided, 'I mean to try. I still feel he was holding something back, not telling me the absolute truth.'

'You can try, he agreed, 'but I think you will be wasting your time.'

'Time?' she reflected. 'I suppose I'm wasting precious time being here with you for my own pleasure, but I have come to terms with that. I'll work all the harder tomorrow.'

They had reached the street and he turned to where they had left the car.

'Where do you mean to go after Salzburg?' he asked.

'I'll have to decide about that after I've seen Sebastian again,' she said as he helped her into the passenger seat. 'If he isn't able to help me—or won't—I'll have to think of something else.'

When they reached the Goldener Hirsch, he stood on the pavement to bid her goodnight.

'You won't come in?' she asked as he glanced at the watch on his wrist.

'If you are determined to be up and about while the dew is still on the grass, I shouldn't keep you!' he said. 'Have a pleasant day tomorrow and remember what I told you about the Residenzplatz cabs!'

The advice, offered with a smile, had the sound of finality about it which she wanted to deny as they stood out there on the deserted pavement with a wayward moon glancing down at them between swiftly moving clouds.

'Stephen,' she said, looking at him directly as she put her arms about his neck, 'thank you for a wonderful day!'

Fleetingly she kissed him, his lips hard under her own, before she turned to run into the searching glare of the bright lights in the hotel foyer where half of Salzburg still seemed to be gathered, laughing the night away.

Next morning she made her way to the Dietrichs' shop once more, but her reception was the same. Hans greeted her with a hesitant smile, stumbling into the back premises to summon his brother, and when Sebastian finally emerged it was to tell her politely that he had nothing to add to his statement of the day before.

'I cannot discuss a former client,' he insisted, 'nor tell you her name. You will understand, I am sure. They may be some other way you can contact your Alice Silton. I wish you well.'

'If you could only tell me where she lived when you last met her, or who her employer was,' Janet persisted. 'I would be more than grateful. Herr Dietrich, because it is important to me to get in touch with her or whoever else might help me to find her. I'm doing this for a very old friend of Alice, who is also my godfather. He wishes to meet her again, if that is at all possible. Any information you would give me would be in the strictest confidence, of course,' she added. 'I would have no reason even to mention your name.'

He regarded her with the deepest understanding in his dark brown eyes.

'I regret that I must refuse,' he repeated. 'You must seek this information elsewhere.'

'Is there somewhere you could suggest?' she asked. 'Without betraying any confidences,' she added a trifle drily.

'None at all,' he answered firmly. 'Perhaps it would be better if you left Salzburg and tried elsewhere.'

Janet sighed.

'Thank you,' she said, knowing that she had come up against the stone wall of his decision. 'I'm sure you would have helped me if you could.'

He looked relieved, watching her go.

Walking back through the crowded arcades and lunching at an open-air restaurant, she decided that the Goldener Hirsch was too expensive, even although Richard had given her *carte blanche* in that respect. If she did stay in Salzburg for another day or two she would find a smaller hotel somewhere on the outskirts of the city, perhaps, which would be more reasonably priced, although she could not just get up and go without seeing Stephen again or leaving a message for him.

She took a cab from the Residenzplatz, sitting back in the dappled sunlight as the little cream horse made its leisurely way through the busy streets, tossing his long white mane back from his head, hoofs clip-clopping gently over the cobbles, the rein held loosely between the cabman's hands. It was what Stephen had recommended, but there was a curiously empty feeling in her heart as she rode along.

When they reached the Goldener Hirsch, she half expected him to be there, although there was no reason why he should be.

'Has there been a message for me?' she found herself asking at reception when she went to collect her key.

'Not this morning,' the clerk told her politely after looking in the pigeon-hole above her room number. 'If anything comes in I'll have it phoned up to your room or paged through the hotel.'

'Thank you.' For a moment she hesitated. 'I'll be checking out tomorrow morning, by the way. Will that be all right?'

'Certainly, madam.' The clerk barely glanced at her. 'Can I find you some accommodation elsewhere in Austria?'

'I'm not quite sure where I shall be going,' she told him truthfully, 'but I shall certainly need a taxi.'

'That can also be arranged,' he decided, noting how disconcerted she looked. 'The head porter will have your luggage brought down as soon as you ring. Have you enjoyed your stay in Salzburg, madam?'

'Very much,' she assured him. 'Very much indeed.'

There was still time to go out in search of alternative accommodation, she decided, since she did not want to eat alone in the hotel, but she found herself wandering in the busy streets again without purpose, unwilling to come to a definite decision. After all, the reception clerk had offered to help her with alternative accommodation, and there was much more to see of Salzburg itself. She would check out in the morning with a clearer head and a diminished sense of disappointment, no doubt.

Drawn back to the Goldener Hirsch with the hope that a message from Stephen had now been left there, she reached the hotel as the sun was setting over the Salzach river. It had been a warm day, full of sunshine, and the trees in the gardens had taken on a fresher green as they burst into new leaf. Only the snow on the distant alps suggested that winter hadn't turned his back completely on the higher slopes where he retained his icy grip.

She paid off her taxi a short distance from the hotel, walking slowly beneath the trees to the main entrance where another taxi was waiting, and beyond it she saw Stephen standing in the doorway with an elegant older woman, obviously escorting her to the waiting cab.

Instinctively she drew back. His companion was arrestingly beautiful even in the rapidly fading light, but she looked delicate, almost frail as he helped her down the steps, the long cloak she wore almost reaching her ankles as she placed one shapely foot before the other and clung to Stephen's arm. At that distance it was impossible to hear their conversation, even if she had wanted to, but what they had to say to each other appeared to be intimate and fond. A tiny gust of laughter floated towards her on the evening breeze, and she watched as they kissed, with a hard lump rising in her throat.

Stephen kissed his companion on both cheeks, as he had kissed her that first night on their return to the Goldener Hirsch, but there seemed to be a different warmth about this present parting. Eager arms went suddenly about his neck as his compion drew his dark head down to the level of her lips where she kissed him in her turn with undoubted affection.

Janet heard them both laughing as he opened the taxi door to help her in, and the brief glance she got of the cab's occupant as she drove away confirmed her belief that this was one of the most beautiful women she had ever seen.

Stephen's secret love?

Walking behind him into the hotel, she knew herself curiously disturbed. She would confirm her departure from the Goldener Hirsch at once and forget all about Stephen Kempson and the magic of a night of stars. She had decided to stay in Salzburg, she told herself, because of her deep conviction that somewhere near at hand was the answer to Richard's hope, that somewhere in the valley of the swift-flowing Saalach she would find another and more substantial clue to Alice Silton's whereabouts, but she had drawn a blank and there was no further need for her to stay.

'What is this I hear?' Stephen had followed her across the busy foyer. 'You are checking out tomorrow. Is your mission, then, completely accomplished?' he demanded.

It was difficult to read the expression in his eyes—surprise, concern or even anger, from which she turned away.

'No,' she said. 'But I've got to find some other, more suitable hotel.' She glanced around the palatial foyer. 'This place is far too expensive for me if I mean to stay in Austria.'

'You're quite sure you have to stay?' he asked, leading her towards a comfortable settee behind an adjacent pillar.

'Absolutely.' She was convinced now. 'Though not necessarily in Salzburg,' she added. 'The Dietrich brothers were my only real contact, and they have refused to help me. I went there again this morning,' she confessed, 'with no different result. They had known Alice in the past but seemed reluctant to talk about her now. Why, I don't know, because it all seems very simple to me. I asked them again to tell me about her employer, but they wouldn't, so I suppose he was someone of importance in the city who might still be a valued customer. Are you remaining in Salzburg?' she asked abruptly, recalling his elegant companion of a few minutes ago who could easily be the 'friend' he was staying with.

'No,' he said. 'I'm moving on.'

This, then, was surely the end of their friendship, the termination of a small romance!

'Tomorrow?' she asked.

He nodded, signalling to a passing waiter.

'Have we still what remains of today?' Janet heard herself asking as something frail seemed to be breaking up inside her—dying, perhaps. 'You've made Salzburg come alive for me.'

'I'd like to take you to the marionette theatre,' he said. 'It is something everyone ought to see.'

'I'd love that! I saw it advertised and it's the sort of thing I like,' she confessed.

'There's also a *Schlosskonzert* in the Residenz, but that might be fully booked,' he added.

'I'll settle for the marionettes,' she told him gaily. 'I think they could be fun!'

'At least you won't have to battle with the language, and the music is generally Mozart.' He glanced at his watch. 'Can you be ready in half an hour?'

'Easily! Will you wait here?'

He nodded, looking across the busy foyer where half Salzburg seemed to be meeting friends and guests to spirit them off to one theatre or another in the true meaning of hospitality. The women ere all beautifully dressed and Janet took several minutes to consider her own wardrobe, telling herself that she could never hope to look as elegant as Stephen's late companion, but at least she could look fresh. In the end she chose the little dinner dress she had worn that first evening on the Orient Express, because it seemed to retain all the glamour and magic of the famous train and their first meal together.

When she went down in the lift with her coat over her arm, Stephen was in conversation with the reception clerk, but he crossed to her side immediately.

'You're exactly a minute late!' he laughed. 'But I'll overlook the fact, just this once!'

'I can only apologise!' she smiled.

'I've hired a taxi because it will be more convenient than taking the car, and we can move on more easily after the show.'

The marionette theatre was an absolute delight to Janet who sat enchanted throughout the show as the little figures were manipulated so skilfully on the tiny stage.

'They're so true to life,' she smiled while Stephen beat time to the music. 'Is Mozart your favourite?'

'More or less. I was brought up with his music, living so near Salzburg, and my mother was always a devotee. She still is,' he added unexpectedly, 'although she doesn't visit the theatre so often these days.'

She wanted to ask more about his mother, to glimpse some

of his childhood background, but after her experience with Sebastian Dietrich she decided against too many questions.

'How thirsty are you?' he asked lightly when the delightful little show was over. 'You can hardly leave Salzburg without a visit to a beer cellar.'

He was expressing the enthusiasm of the perfect host, although occasionally when she looked at him his expression seemed guarded. It was a mad adventure, she told herself, but this man's magnetism could not be denied, even if underneath his smile lay the suggestion of a deliberate purpose which she chose not to examine too closely. Everything else about their relationship seemed perfect.

'Why did you come to see Richard when you were in London?' she asked. 'I feel I should have tried to help when we first met, but you were slightly off-putting, you know. Brusque and to the point. It was Richard Cosgrave you had come to see, and not his secretary, who couldn't possibly deal with what you wanted to know!'

'Is that how it seemed?' he asked. 'I believe I did think along those lines, but then, I didn't really know you—how dedicated you could be to a cause and how tenacious.'

'That is just being practical,' she protested. 'Part of my training.'

'Which is the usual excuse of the career woman!'

She considered him carefully, the firm mouth and craggy chin which made his own determination plain.

'I've never considered myself as a career woman. Not the "sacrificing everything for successs" type, anyway, because so often they throw away the chance of ultimate happiness without really knowing why.'

'What is ultimate happiness in your opinion?' he asked idly. 'A home and family, with a nice warm fire to sit beside when the wind blows cold outside?'

'I could settle for that,' she agreed, 'but I don't think I'm ready for it yet because I still wonder where life might be taking me. I suppose if I had some outstanding talent to offer an appreciative world I might think differently, but I'm very ordinary. I'm not unhappy in my work—I have a lot going for me—and Richard has provided a comfortable home for me, so perhaps I feel I should—recompense him in some way.'

'Like helping him to find the girl he ought to have married thirty years ago?'

The question was terse, the dark frown back between his brows.

'It would mean so much to him to find Alice Silton,' she said, hoping for a measure of his understanding.

'To make amends for deserting her so long ago?'

Astonished at the sudden bitterness of his tone, she turned to face him.

'It wasn't quite like that,' she said. 'They had never actually spoken about marriage because he had so little to offer. They were so very young—both students when they first met, and I suppose he lacked courage or faith in his own ability to succeed. And Alice had a chance to follow her own exciting career which she had worked for over several years. I think they quarrelled about that, not too violently, maybe, but with a finality which sent Alice off to Paris to study while Richard believed himself abandoned by her in London. Why they never wrote to each other afterwards, I can't imagine,' she added thoughtfully. 'Pride could have come into it, or some other reason best known to themselves.'

'Success isn't important,' he said briskly. 'Some people can handle it without it upsetting them; others find it impossible.'

'What have you found, Stephen?' she asked.

He looked across the crowded beer cellar.

'A little of both,' he confessed. 'My mother was a successful woman, but it didn't make her difficult. I remember my childhood as completely uncomplicated, although she had a lot to do, such as shouldering burdens which were a lot too heavy for her and trying to bring me up without a father to lead the way and share responsibility. I can never thank her enough for that.'

'Perhaps that's what makes some of us afraid of marriage—the new generation, I mean. The responsibility bit,' she added slowly. 'Do we shy away from it because we are half afraid?'

'I think we take it in our stride, more or less, and do what we have to do.' He looked across the table at her in the candle-light. 'Do you want to find another hotel in Salzburg, or would a country place suit you just as well?'

'I must look further afield now,' she decided. 'After all, that's why I'm here.' She paused for a moment before she added, 'Richard mentioned a place called Uttendorf somewhere near here. Do you know it?'

His mouth hardened.

'You'll be going back on your tracks,' he said, 'but no matter. I can easily take you there,' he offered after the barest pause. 'It's on the far side of the Thurn Pass and I have—a friend who runs an hotel up there near Ferleiten. I could arrange for you to stay there.'

Her heart leapt in sudden quick response.

'If you are sure? It could be taking you out of your way,' she suggested.

'Not a great deal,' he answered. 'I often go there.'

'Stephen,' she said gratefully, 'you are being very kind. I wonder why.'

He laughed.

'Perhaps because I don't want to part with you,' he suggested drily.

'Now you're being cynical!' she laughed. 'But if you are sure,' she repeated, giving him a chance to reverse a decision which had seemed almost reluctant, 'I'll be happy to accept, although I could easily make my own way to Uttendorf since I have apparently drawn a blank in Salzburg.'

'What contact have you in Uttendorf?' he enquired, ignoring her offer of a retraction. 'It is much more isolated than Salzburg, and only a fraction of the size.'

'You know it quite well? In that case, you might be able to help me,' she suggested.

In the candlelight his face seemed to change, taking on a darkness which caused her heart to beat faster as she waited for his reply.

'I've offered to find you somewhere to stay,' he said. 'Nothing more. What you do with your time in Uttendorf will depend on what you hope to find there.'

'I hope to find Alice Silton or someone who knows where she is now. There was a card addressed to a friend in Paris whom Richard was able to trace—someone who wanted to help—but he went to Australia and they lost touch. It may not be much to go on, but the card was posted in Uttendorf so I have to go there. Why do you smile?' she asked when his eyes glinted in the candlelight. 'Do you think I'm embarking on a wild-goose chase?'

'I think you may be following a cold trail,' he told her succinctly. 'There are two Uttendorfs, you know, and this could be the wrong one.'

'Stephen,' she said, 'I have to try. I've accepted your offer to find me accommodation for a few days but I won't bother you further. I won't involve you in any way.'

'Perhaps I am already involved,' he said, pushing back his chair. 'Shall we go?'

Outside in the cold night she turned up the collar of her woollen coat, shivering a little as they made their way to the Goldener Hirsch. The city lights and the distant stars above them were very bright, but the night wind had come down from the moutains with a touch of ice in its breath.

'I'll pick you up in the morning at ten o'clock,' he offered. 'Be ready!'

He did not kiss her goodnight as she had half expected, and there was no reason for her to feel disappointed, she told herself, but something had gone out of the night, some glow of warmth which had been with her for the greater part of the day. Through the heavy glass door she saw him turn immediately to walk back by the way they had come. It was past midnight, but the city lights still glittered along the narrow streets and above the shadowy arcades, casting a blurred yellow glow into the sky over the Salzach river as it wound darkly between the hills. She looked beyond it to the faint outline of distant alps ghostly white against a darkened sky, wondering what tomorrow's journey would bring.

In the morning, however, she found herself completing her packing with renewed eagerness. It was a new day and one which might bring her a step nearer to success! She had drawn a blank in Salzburg, but perhaps she would come nearer to Alice on the other side of the Kitzbühler.

The morning was brilliant, the sun shining in through her bedroom window like a promise as she rang for a porter to collect her luggage and hurried through her breakfast so that she would not be late for her rendezvous with someone who was really no more than a stranger to her. It was even on the cards that he would not turn up at all, although she dismissed the disconcerting thought immediately.

He came across the foyer as she was settling her account.

'I take it you've had some breakfast,' he said. 'Did you sleep well?'

'Until eight o'clock!' She smiled up at him. 'It must have been all that Mozart and the marionettes, and I didn't even have a single dream!'

He picked up her coat from the chair where she had left it, signalling for her luggage to be carried out as she followed him to the door. Out in the sunshine the Mercedes was waiting, familiar now that they had used it so often.

'Do you have to return it to Innsbruck?' she asked as he helped her into the passenger seat.

'I'm keeping it for another week,' he said, turning to tip the porter who had stowed her case into the capacious boot with his own luggage. 'Then I can turn it in here when I have no more use for it.'

She wanted to ask him other, more personal questions, but decided against curiosity since he appeared to resent it. This was the start of a new day and perhaps a new experience.

The Mercedes ran smoothly, covering the miles with ease, but by the time they had reached St Johann and begun to climb on the road to Kitzbühel the way ahead looked formidable. The snow had not yet left these high places and a thin mist veiled the sky as they drove through the valley, blotting out the sun.

'How disappointing!' Janet sighed. 'It started off so brightly in Salzburg.'

'It's often like this,' he told her, 'then suddenly it will clear. You may find by the time we reach Kitzbühel the sun has come out and and the sky will be clear. I'll phone ahead from there and make our reservations,' he decided.

Janet gave her whole attention to the misty landscape, exclaiming as alp after alp appeared in ghostly splendour on either side of the road for her enchantment. But for the mist it would have been a fairy-tale place full of mysteries to which Stephen Kempson appeared to hold the key.

Before they had reached the ski resort the sun had come out as he had promised, and she sat forward in her seat with renewed eagerness for her first glimpse of the little town.

The snow had almost disappeared from the busy main street, but Stephen drove slowly to avoid the few late winter sports enthusiasts still walking purposefully towards the ski-lifts which would take them up higher to more exciting slopes.

'Most of the shops are putting up their shutters now for the short break between the winter skiing and the summer climbing,' he explained. 'The valley can look ghostly at this time of the year, but I like it best this way.'

She could well imagine him skiing up there on the high

slopes, alone or with a responsible partner who could match his ability on the snow, someone born in this high country, perhaps, whom he had known for most of his life, and inevitably she found herself thinking about his companion of the day before, the elegant woman in grey who had kissed him so tenderly before they had parted at the Goldener Hirsch.

At the far end of the main street he drew up before a large hostelry where several booted and anorak-clad holidaymakers were passing the time drinking coffee or mulled wine while they recounted their adventures on the piste.

'It's noisy in here but incredibly warm,' he commented, 'and you must be ready for something hot to drink. I can recommend the wine if you feel that way inclined.'

'I'd prefer coffee,' she decided, following him into the cosy bar. 'Will you telephone from here?'

'Right away,' he said, 'although we don't need to worry about our accommodation at the *schloss*. It will be practically empty by now.'

'You're going to stay there, too?' she asked, agreeably surprised and excited at the prospect.

'It was once my home,' he said, 'but now it is an efficiently run hotel.' When he saw her surprise he added, 'Even a small *schloss* needs a lot of upkeep, and my mother is far from wealthy.'

'Do you mean she runs the hotel?'

He found an empty table in an alcove.

'She did until a year ago when arthritis got the better of her and she had to seek help,' he explained.

'Won't it seem strange to her—your bringing me here when you know so little about me?' she asked.

He smiled as the waiter came to take his order.

'I know a little more about you than I did in London,' he pointed out. 'It was a long journey on the Orient Express.'

She could not read his expression clearly in the dimness of the raftered bar, but she imagined that his smile was slightly ironic as he looked across the wooden table into her eyes.

'My mother is no longer at the *schloss*,' he said, 'so you needn't worry on that account. I saw her in Salzburg yesterday where she is staying at the Carlton taking the cure. She swears by the mud baths, and I honestly do believe they give her some relief, although I imagine the rest does her even more good in the end.'

This was a new slant to her journey into the mountains, a completely unexpected turn in her quest for Richard's former love, and a tantalising glimpse into Stephen Kempson's past. While she waited for their coffee to be served he went out into the entrance lobby to phone the *schloss*, and she looked about her with renewed interest.

The little hostelry was filling up and the sound of laughter drifted with the smoke among the rafters as friend greeted friend in the camaraderie of the snowfields. If you didn't ski up here, Janet thought, you would be very lonely.

Stephen strode back across the room, tall and distinguished-looking among the bearded denizens of the wine bar.

'It's all arranged,' he said. 'You are certain of a night's lodgings, at least.'

'I feel I'm intruding, almost asking you to help,' she protested. 'But please feel free to leave me at the *schloss* if you want to go on.'

'I couldn't do that, could I?' he said. 'Not after bringing you all this way.'

'Stephen——' She hesitated, the colour rising in her cheeks. 'Supposing I have to stay? For more than just one night, I mean.'

'That, too, can be arranged,' he decided as coffee-pots and cups were set before them. 'The *schloss* is run quite efficiently, I can assure you.'

The thought of their destination intrigued her as she poured strong, black coffee into their cups.

'Milk?' he asked, taking up the second pot. 'We have a fair

way to go.'

'I was going to ask about that,' she admitted. 'How far is it to the *schloss*?'

'About another hour on the far side of the pass.' He pushed the sugar bowl towards her. 'There's no hope of another meal till we get there.'

'You make it all sound very—isolated,' she suggested, 'but I suppose that is part of its attraction for you.'

'It has also brought my mother the necessary visitors she needs,' he pointed out. 'When the summer season starts in earnest the Schloss Erlach can be a very busy place.'

'I can hardly wait till we get there!' she exclaimed, stirring sugar into her coffee. 'It will be an entirely new experience for me.'

He looked beyond her across the crowded tavern.

'Don't expect too much,' he warned. 'We're not at all grand.'

She smiled.

'Please let me have my little romance!' she begged. 'It's not every day one can put up in a castle.'

'You could be disappointed,' he warned, 'but I won't try to disenchant you. The *schloss* is, I suppose, a castle in miniature, but there are hundreds of them scattered around in this part of the world, and not all of them beautiful.'

'Is the Schloss Erlach beautiful?' she wanted to know.

He considered the question for a moment, sipping his coffee.

'Grim would be a better word,' he decided. 'Certainly in the winter.'

'You disappoint me!'

'I'm sorry,' he apologised. 'I didn't know you were looking for beauty. The *schloss* has a lot of character, but it is set too high for beauty. As a matter of fact, it looks like part of the rock face from a distance, although it improves on closer inspection. I think you will like it.'

When they were back on the road again, climbing through

the pass with the massif of the Kitzbühler on either side, it seemed as if they were closed into another world of white mountain peaks with a clear blue sky above them. The magic of the snow-covered heights took hold of her, while Stephen's sudden preoccupation only seemed to be part of the silence. He drove purposefully, knowing the road from boyhood, and his dark profile silhouetted against the snow might have been carved from the rock beyond. A man, Janet thought, who would not forgive an injury easily, a man whose standards were as firm as the rock on either side of the high pass through which they travelled. She thought of Richard and why Stephen had travelled to London to meet him. He hadn't trusted her with the reason for his visit, but somehow she thought it might be personal. In the usual business way Stephen could have been expected to confide in her as Richard's deputy, or even to consult with Nigel Bannister, who was a capable substitute for his employer on most occasions.

The high snowfields were a magnificent sight with the April sun on them and, once through the pass, they were in a vast land of sparkling blue glaciers and rushing mountain streams overflowing with melting ice water from the mountain slopes above. As far as the eyes could see there seemed to be no sign of human habitation, save for a few mountain huts high in the snow.

'It's hard to believe that anywhere could be so remote,' she said, feasting her eyes on the sparkling whiteness all around her. 'Or that anyone lives here,' she added doubtfully.

'Quite a few people do, and in the summer the valleys are hives of activity with climbers everywhere.' Stephen turned his attention back to the road as he drove into Mittersill, following a narrow track along the bank of a swollen river into the valley through which it flowed. 'Most of the houses in the vicinity cater for the heavy-boot brigade,' he added. 'They come in all shapes and sizes, fully equipped or not, to tackle the mountains for their varying reasons, and generally they go back satisfied. Many of them come to the *schloss* year after year, but now it is the slack season and we have the mountains practically to ourselves.'

That was why he liked to come to the Schloss Erlach at this time of the year, Janet decided, to feel that this glorious world of snow-clad mountains and azure sky was his and his alone. Or was there some other reason lurking in the depths of these darkly penetrating eyes?

'You can see the *schloss* when we turn the next bend,' he told her, giving his full attention to the winding track. 'Over there, to the left.'

Janet was never to forget her first sight of the Schloss Erlach. It stood on a small raised plateau above the track with a mountain river gushing beneath it and April sunshine gilding its walls. In a poor light it might have looked grey and uninviting, but in full sun, with its mullioned windows flashing back the light, it was the most exciting place she had ever seen.

'You haven't done it justice,' she accused as Stephen put the Mercedes to the slope of the hill. 'It's—out of a fairy-tale!'

He laughed at her enthusiasm.

'You're a romantic,' he said, 'and I don't suppose you'll ever be cured.'

'I don't want to be,' she told him simply. 'It must be awful to see everything in a dim, grey light.'

'The *schloss* can look like that quite often.' His mouth was suddenly grim. 'When the wind blows cold over it you could imagine it as Dracula's castle, and sometimes it is almost obliterated by driving snow. Even that, of course, can have its own attraction, and I've been known to prefer it that way.'

Janet looked up at the *schloss*. Stephen had prepared her for its smallness, but not for the quality of remoteness and peace which surrounded it. Even if she drew another blank in these wonderful surroundings, she felt that the short time she would spend in this odd little castle would be productive in so many ways.

As they approached the plateau, a slight figure in bright red skied past them, waving in greeting as Stephen slowed the car.

'That must be Sophia,' he decided. 'I hadn't any idea she would be up here.'

The slim red figure reversed her progress down the slope, turning to follow the car as they reached the entrance to the *schloss*. Looking back at her with some curiosity, Janet took her for a child, a young teenager, perhaps, whose great enthusiasm was the snow, but when she drew up alongside she looked considerably older. Stephen stopped the car.

'This is my cousin by marriage,' he introduced her. 'Sophia, this is Miss Blair from London. I phoned from Kitzbühel to make a reservation for her while she is in the district.'

Janet's gaze encountered eyes that were distinctly hostile, brown eyes fringed by thick, dark lashes which were Sophia's only asset. Her stubborn mouth and small, sharp nose gave her the look of an inquisitive bird, and there was nothing to be seen of her hair tucked into a red woollen hood but a few loose, wispy strands of black which the wind had whipped across her face in her energetic downhill flight. She smoothed them back to look at Janet, who suddenly felt the interloper.

'There won't be much for you to do here,' she said in almost faultless English. 'You're too late for any serious skiing and too early for climbing.'

'I don't ski,' Janet was forced to admit, feeling inadequate, 'and I hadn't thought of climbing, although it must be wonderful. I came to Salzburg—on business.'

Without replying, Sophia turned her attention to Stephen.

'You have managed to return at last!' she exclaimed, her eyes glowing. 'How glad I am! It will be like old times once more now that you are here. The *schloss* is almost empty.' She gave Janet a brief glance. 'Soon we shall have it to ourselves.'

Stephen let in the clutch, driving slowly the few hundred

yards to the *schloss* where Sophia discarded her red skis in the snow and stood waiting. As soon as her cousin was out of the car she flung her arms about his neck.

'Why have you stayed away so long?' she demanded, kissing him on the lips. 'I have watched for your return for weeks, but now you have left it too late to go off into the moutains to ski!'

'I apologise,' he said, returning her kiss. 'I hadn't intended to stay away so long, but you know I have a living to make.'

'Oh—Paris!' his cousin by marriage exclaimed. 'I have no patience with large cities. They bore me, Stevie, quite a lot. I have had enough of them—Paris and Vienna and London—and now we are going once again to London because my mother enjoys it there.'

'There's no reason why you shouldn't enjoy it, too,' he said, turning to help Janet out of the car. 'There are plenty of things to do in London, I can assure you.'

'You wouldn't say that if you were with my mother and Wolf all the time,' Sophia pointed out. 'It's all so deadly dull, and I can never go anywhere alone. Why don't you come with us?' she demanded.

'I may even do that,' Stephen decided after a moment's pause. 'I may have some unfinished business to see to in London. I'm glad Wolf is going with you.'

'Mother insists.' Sophia's eyes were full on Janet now. 'Wolf is her willing slave, someone she can order about as she pleases, someone who will obey her every command.'

'You're making it all sound so disgustingly feudal,' Stephen laughed. 'Wolf owes a lot to your mother, remember, and he is more than willing to serve her in return.'

'*Serve* being the operative word.' Sophia's mouth turned down at the corners. 'I have grown to hate him.'

'Don't be absurd!' Stephen put a protective arm about her shoulders. 'He'd serve you as willingly as he serves your mother, if that's what you really want.'

'I don't! I think he is—repulsive, but everything will be

changed now that you are back. He will no longer be my gaoler when I have you to turn to,' Sophia declared.

'I can see I shouldn't have stayed away so long!' Stephen was taking his cousin's complaints quite lightly, which Janet thought was a mistake. She could see that his enforced absence was too long for the volatile young woman who still viewed her with suspicion as they moved across the trampled snow to enter the *schloss*, and that might be dangerous. So young and impressionable, Sophia was Stephen's great admirer, just as Wolf seemed to be in thrall to her mother, who awaited them inside the *schloss*.

'Mama will not be pleased that you have given her so little notice of your arrival,' Sophia told him.

'That is no matter,' Stephen decided almost arrogantly. 'You are an hotel now and should be glad of extra guests, especially at the close of the season.'

Sophia stuck her skis into the snow.

'That's beside the point,' she said. 'We're fully booked for the summer when we return from London.'

The heavy door of the *schloss* was closed against them, but it seemed to Janet that they were already being watched. Sophia pulled the ancient bell.

'Wolf will answer,' she said. 'He has nothing else to do.'

Slowly the door opened to reveal the serving man, who was very much younger than Janet had expected.

'Why do you bolt the door, Wolf?' Sophia demanded. 'It is a great nuisance having always to ring the bell.'

Wolf regarded her disdainfully.

'It is on your mother's orders,' he informed her. 'You should obey her more often yourself.'

Sophia laughed.

'This is Wolf, our gaoler,' she said to Janet. 'He will do everything he can to help you.'

The sarcasm in her voice was not lost on Wolf, nor on Stephen, who walked inside in Janet's wake.

'I'll have your luggage sent up to your room,' he said. 'I'm sure you will be comfortable.'

A shadow moved among the deeper shadows at the back of the hall as a velvet hanging was suddenly disturbed, and Janet found herself looking towards it with a hint of trepidation in her heart, knowing that Sophia's mother was waiting there. Stephen took a step forward.

'Hello, Aunt Anastasia!' he said. 'I'm sorry we could not have given you more warning—all this was arranged on the spur of the moment. Miss Blair found the Goldener Hirsch rather expensive for a long stay and, since she is going to Uttendorf to make some enquiries, I suggested she should come here.'

Janet found herself confronted by a big, Teutonic-looking woman in her early fifties, her raven-black hair coiled in a sort of coronet high on her head, her heavy shoulders stooped a little as if the weight of so much hair was almost too much for them to support. Heavy cheekbones dominated her gaunt face and gimlet blue eyes appeared to miss nothing as she greeted her unexpected guest with unconcealed suspicion.

'You would have been better accommodated in Kitzbühel or Innsbruck,' she declared. 'We are about to close. It is the end of the winter season when we take a vacation before the summer visitors arrive.'

Janet was beginning to wish that she hadn't allowed Stephen to persuade her to come here where there was no real welcome.

'You will not go to London till the beginning of May,' Stephen pointed out. 'Or so my mother thought when I met her in Salzburg.'

Anastasia Waldburger was instantly silenced by the brief remark.

'You will sign the register,' she said to Janet, 'and I will show you to your room.'

Stephen surrendered her luggage to the ever-helpful Wolf, who carried it purposefully to the wide oak stairway at the far side of the hall. He wore a green baize apron over a white shirt, with cord knickerbockers in a paler shade of green, and Janet thought with amusement that all he needed to complete the picture was a Tyrolean hat with a feather in it, which he probably had stored away somewhere for those outdoor activities which took him on important journeys with his overpowering mistress or her impressionable child.

Yet Sophia was hardly a child, she thought as she signed her name in the register, adding her nationality and her place of residence for Anastasia's scrutiny at a more convenient time.

Following the grim custodian of the Schloss Erlach towards the staircase, she was able to glance at Stephen where he stood on the other side of the hall, imagining a sudden ruthlessness about him which was difficult to credit. He had thrown his mother's name into the conversation deliberately to remind Anastasia Waldburger that she did not own the *schloss*, although he hadn't treated her in any servile way, and all this was surely a recipe for trouble in the future.

CHAPTER THREE

JANET had been given a room overlooking the valley and the winding river that ran through it, a turbulent stream swollen by the water from the melting snowfields all around it. It was a sun-filled room at that time of day, full of golden light, and her heart lifted a little as she began to unpack, hanging her clothes on the padded hangers in the heavy black oak wardrobe which took up most of the space along one wall. All the furniture in the room was heavy and dark, including the massive four-poster bed with its green brocade canopy which stood against another wall and seemed to dominate the entire room. A carved chest was to serve her as a dressing-table and a second door led into a shower-room where towels had been laid out for her use, heavy towels striped in green and red which reminded her of Anastasia Waldburger when she had first encountered her.

She showered, changed, and was combing her hair into some sort of order when a light tap on the door took her across the room to answer it. Her unexpected visitor was Stephen.

'Are you happy with the view?' he asked, coming into the room without invitation.

'I've never slept in a four-poster before!' Janet smiled, unexpectedly happy that she would be staying at the *schloss* for at least a day or two to further her search for Alice Silton. 'It's all in the right key, Stephen, this wonderful old *schloss* in such beautiful surroundings. You must have had a very happy childhood here. What made you settle for Paris?'

'Because I was born there,' he said briefly. 'I got away as often as I could, of course, and this was the ideal place for a holiday. My mother worked here.'

'Oh?'

She had wondered about the *schloss* and his mother's connection with it, but he refused to answer her unspoken question, crossing instead to the long window which dominated the valley below.

'There are still a few guests left,' he told her. 'Two Italians from Milan, I understand, and a couple from Munich who come every year. They are all enthusiastic skiers, so I don't think you'll see very much of them while the good snow lasts.'

'Have you come to ski?' she asked.

'Not exclusively, although it's hard to resist a run out on a good day like this.'

'Sophia will be disappointed if you don't stay,' she mused. 'She seems a real enthusiast.'

'Dyed in the wool!' he agreed. 'Don't let her tempt you out if you don't want to go,' he warned. 'There are no real nursery slopes up here for a beginner.'

'I'll remember that,' she assured him. 'Besides, I'm not here to ski or even to learn.'

'No,' he said, crossing to the door. 'When do you intend to go to Uttendorf?'

'As soon as possible.' She remembered the comparative isolation of their present situation. 'Stephen, where can I hire a car?'

'You can't. Not here, anyway,' he told her, 'but if you are not in too great a hurry I can take you tomorrow.'

'You put me very firmly in your debt,' she acknowledged. 'Are you going to Uttendorf on your own account?'

'I'm going back to Salzburg,' he said, 'by a more direct route. Amazingly, it goes through Uttendorf!'

'Thank you,' she said. 'You're very thoughtful.'

He closed the door gently behind him and she heard him go down the uncarpeted stairs to the hall, where Sophia's laughter greeted him like a peal of bells.

Reluctant to rejoin them so quickly, she finished her unpacking, standing afterwards to look down on the narrow valley below her window. The river was in spate, flowing swiftly, with little cataracts foaming on its surface as it jumped over boulders or leapt against the bank where snow still lay in deep patches, not yet willing to accept that spring had come at last. Farther up the valley everything was white where winter retained his grip, and the heavily scored ski-trails suggested that the higher slopes where still in use. As she watched, someone in a red ski-suit appeared on the terrace beneath her. It was Sophia, retrieving the skis she had stuck into the snow an hour ago. Surely she wasn't going out again?

At that point she heard voices, someone calling back into the *schloss*, and presently Stephen came out to join his cousin. 'My cousin by marriage', he had called the girl who was so obviously attracted to him, but he had shown her no more than brotherly affection when she had greeted him so enthusiastically down there on the terrace where the Mercedes still stood in the dancing sunlight. He moved towards the car while their conversation continued, and it was obvious that he intended to drive away. Sophia snatched her skis from the banked snow, kicking one foot into place before he could help her.

Janet drew back from the window, but not before she had seen him bend down to help his cousin with the second ski. When Sophia straightened, leaning heavily on her sticks, she looked disappointed and genuinely angry, shaking off the helping hand he had placed beneath her elbow as she tightened the belt she wore round her waist. Like a slim red arrow she shot off, scorning the road as she took to the nearest ski-run, while Stephen gazed after her with a thoughtful look in his eyes. He feels responsible, Janet thought, and it was the sort of reaction she would have expected of him.

When she went down the staircase into the raftered hall, he was standing beside the open fireplace at its far end, his brows gathered in a dark frown as he contemplated the blazing logs burning in the wrought-iron fire-basket, but when he heard her footsteps on the polished wood floor he turned immediately to welcome her.

'Come and get warm,' he invited, 'and then we can have something to eat. My aunt has gone to see about it.'

'Are we late—or early?' Janet asked. 'When does she generally prepare lunch?'

'She doesn't. Most of our guests prefer a packed meal in the middle of the day to take on to the slopes, especially when they are going fairly far afield. There are good runs on this side of the Zillertaler and through the Hohe Jallern for experienced skiers like Sophia, for example.' He smiled as he kicked a log into place, watching the sparks fly up the wide stone chimney into the cold, still air beyond. 'Sophia is a bit of a crackpot where skiing is concerned,' he added. 'She lives for it and she would be out there on the snow every day if she had her own way, but her mother thinks she should earn her keep now and then.'

'What does she do?' Janet asked.

He shrugged.

'She trained as a secretary in Munich and she is good with languages, but she hasn't yet found a permanent job. That's why my aunt feels she should help in the house while she remains here.'

Janet could imagine Anastasia Waldburger laying down the law in that respect in no uncertain terms, and obviously her wayward daughter was often brought to heel.

'We must be giving your aunt a lot of trouble preparing an extra meal,' she suggested. 'Would it be any use if I offered to help?'

'None at all,' he laughed. 'Aunt Anastasia would take it as an insult, a slight on her ability to cope. She's that sort of person.'

'Oh, dear!' Janet exclaimed. 'I *have* given you a problem.'

'Don't worry about it,' he advised, making room for her at

the fire. 'Anastasia couldn't live without problems. It's her nature to feel aggrieved.'

'Is there a Herr Waldburger?'

He shook his head.

'He died many years ago, leaving Anastasia with Sophia to bring up on very little money, I'm afraid. He was a quiet man—a dreamer, I suppose you might say—and he expected Anastasia to order their life, which she did. He relied on her for most things and when he died she was well equipped to manage her own life, except for the money they didn't have. That has always been a sore point with my aunt, together with the fact that she felt shut out from her former home here at the *schloss*. She was a Von Erlach by right—by birth, anyway,' he conceded, 'and I think it still rankles that my mother married her brother so soon before his death. The Baron was my mother's second husband, and my stepfather, and he had been blind for a very long time. He, too, was a quiet man, not at all like Anastasia, but I'm sure he was a happy one.'

Janet gazed down at the burning logs in the lovely wrought-iron fire-basket, realising that it was so much in keeping with everything else in the *schloss*. Wrought-iron candelabra stood on the polished floor where lovely old Persian rugs made dark splashes on the lighter pine, and a great wrought-iron basket lay ready to hand, full of logs to replenish the leaping fire.

'It reminds me of Sebastian Dietrich's shop,' she mused. 'There were so many lovely things there, I felt that I could have browsed in it all day.'

'Yes,' he said flatly, looking beyond her as heavy footsteps crossed the uncovered floor between the rugs and Anastasia came towards them.

'Your meal is ready,' she announced distantly. 'I have set it in the breakfast-room.'

'We must be giving you a lot of extra work,' Janet said. 'We should have had something to eat in Kitzbühel.'

Anastasia froze her with a look.

'It is my job,' she declared with more than a hint of ice in her voice. 'I am used to it. Come this way.'

Janet went with her across the hall, glad that she was not alone as Stephen followed her. In the small breakfast-room a round table had been drawn up close to a wood stove where more logs burned, and a white tablecloth was set with two places facing each other. No concession here to the labour-saving table mats, she thought as Stephen held out a chair for her. It would not be Anastasia's way, because everything would have to be done as it had been when when she had lived here at the *schloss* many years ago. In her youth, table mats would have been frowned upon and no amount of extra work laundering the lovely old linen would be grudged nor even thought about.

The table had been elaborately set with heavy silver and fine china, while the sun streaming in through the latticed window-panes brought out a thousand dancing lights in the crystal goblets at either place. While his aunt served the soup, Stephen considered the wine.

'If there's anything else you wish to drink,' his aunt suggested, 'I can have it brought up from the cellar.'

'This will do nicely,' he assured her. 'Your soup always smells delicious!'

'I hope it also tastes well,' Anastasia returned. 'As you know, it is made each day—for dinner in the evening.'

Having made her point, she strode off to supervise the rest of their meal.

'I feel terribly guilty,' Janet apologised again. 'We could have eaten at Kitzbühel, Stephen, and got here later in the day.'

'I thought you would like to see the *schloss* at its best,' he reflected, 'without a horde of anorak-clad enthusiasts stamping all over the place.'

'The heavy-booted brigade!' she laughed. 'Stephen, I'd love

to be able to ski. There must be a freedom up there on the high slopes you can't convey to anyone who has never been, but I suppose I have arrived too late to try.'

'Much too late,' he agreed. 'Besides, you have other work to do.' He looked at her across the spotless cloth. 'What will happen if you *don't* find Alice Silton?' he enquired.

'I'll have to go home with my tail between my legs,' she laughed. 'But I don't mean to fail, Stephen. I have to go on trying because of Richard, and I expect you understand that.'

His mouth firmed to a hard line.

'I have tried to,' he said, 'and now I must accept what you intend to do. We'll set out fairly early tomorrow and I'll drop you in Uttendorf on my way to Salzburg.'

She wondered why he was going back to Salzburg so quickly, but no doubt it was to see the lovely, elegant woman he had kissed so tenderly in the hotel doorway. A sharp little pain touched her heart as she looked at him, but he neither confirmed nor denied her supposition as a young table-maid come in with a soup tureen and two warm bowls. He spoke to her in German, asking her how she was.

'Very well!' the buxom young woman returned in the language she was so eager to learn. 'You see I speak the English now quite good!'

Stephen nodded.

'You will soon be better at it than Sophia,' he said diplomatically as she served their soup.

'You think so? That is pleasing me very much. I am taking lessons with a tape recorder. Do you know what I mean?'

'Perfectly. But you have a good teacher in Wolf.'

'Oh, Wolf!' She blushed. 'He has no time to teach when he is always so busy.'

'Obeying my aunt,' Stephen supplemented as she left the room. 'Anastasia makes quite sure everyone knows their place. Even me,' he added whimsically. 'She thinks I have no real right to come back here now that I am working for myself.'

'Or bring a stranger with you?'

'That, too,' he acknowledged. 'It will take her some time to accept you.'

'I won't be here for very long,' she reminded him. 'Not much more than a day or two. I would have liked to have met your mother,' she added spontaneously.

He broke a bread roll on the plate beside his soup, not answering her immediately.

'I think you might have got on well together,' he decided at last. 'My mother is still very English, in spite of the fact that she has lived so long in Austria. She married for a second time quite late in life, and the Baron was much older, but they were very happy together through their common love of music. They had many other things in common, of course, and she nursed him faithfully through the final stages of his illness. She came here originally to help with a composition he was working on when he discovered he was going blind and, after many years, when she knew he was dying and needed her comfort and care, she married him.'

Sudden tears stung at the back of Janet's eyes for a moment as she waited for him to continue.

'I've a strong feeling that she made her decision to remarry because of me,' he said slowly. 'I'd had a ragged sort of childhood moving with her from place to place after my father died, and I know she made many sacrifices during those years. We were never very well off because she never really made her mark in the musical world. She had a sweet voice, but it was not powerful enough for opera and so she picked up the odd job where she could to make sure of my education. I owe her a great deal,' he concluded, 'and now that she is sick I have to look after her in my turn.'

Anastasia came in with the main course, carrying the tray as if she were serving at a banquet.

'I could not give you a great deal of choice,' she complained, 'with such short notice, but you will eat again in the evening when the others have returned.'

She placed a casserole dish on the table between them.

'This looks splendid,' Stephen acknowledged.

'Do you wish to be served, or will you take what you want?' she asked. 'I'm sure there will be plenty.'

The stout little table-maid appeared with the vegetables, placing the tureen in front of Janet with a nervous smile.

'It is very hot,' she announced. 'I will now take the top for you.'

Lifting the lid with the white towel she carried, she waited for Janet to deal with the vegetables.

'Whether you want them or not, you'd better eat them,' Stephen advised under his breath. 'She probably prepared them herself.'

'Cabbage?' Janet asked, passing him the dish. 'I hope we can eat again by eight o'clock!'

Their meal was completed by a delightful apple strudel served with thick, rich cream.

'Do you always eat as well as this in Austria?' Janet demanded.

'Generally,' he admitted. 'Wait till you've been out in the fresh air for a couple of hours and you'll begin to wonder if you've eaten since yesterday! Would you like to walk,' he added, 'since you can't ski?'

'Could I try to ski?' she asked hopefully. 'Please, Stephen! It may be my only opportunity.'

He hesitated for a moment.

'Why not?' he decided. 'You can borrow a pair of Sophia's skis.'

'Would she agree to that? Janet asked doubtfully.

'I should think so, if she knew how keen you are!' he laughed.

'I'm not too well equipped,' she told him when she returned to the hall an hour later in her only pair of slacks and the one thick woollen sweater she had packed against the cold.

'We must find you a pair of boots,' he suggested. 'That's the main thing, though you can't fall about in the snow in such flimsy trousers. In fact, if you manage the lower ski-trail without a mishap, I'll be satisfied,' he added critically.

'You're joking!'

He had knelt to adjust her skis and suddenly he looked up into her laughing eyes.

'Believe me,' he said, 'I'm not. I don't want you to spend the next few weeks here with a broken leg.'

He meant what he said. He didn't want the responsibility of her being forced to remain at the *schloss* because of an injury. Perhaps he didn't want her there at all. Why, then, had he invited her into the mountains—into his former home—while she continued her search for Alice Silton?

'Ready?' he asked as he stepped into his own skis. 'We'll take it cautiously.'

They went together down the gentle slope from the *schloss* while the keen air bit into her cheeks, turning them rosy red. Doing all the wrong things in spite of his expert guidance, she felt that his patience wouldn't last very long.

'I expect you're either a natural at this or you're not,' she observed breathlessly. 'I'm absolutely terrified!'

He drew up beside her.

'Don't be,' he advised. 'Otherwise you'll never learn. It takes a lot of practice, but afterwards you'll enjoy every minute of it.'

'Even when I fall on my face?'

'Don't expect to, and don't grab your sticks as if you were clinging to the edge of the world. Here, let me show you!' He came to stand close beside her, guiding her hands. 'You'll feel most of the strain in your knees and thighs, but that will pass. Learn to crawl before you walk, and you won't go far wrong!' He released her but did not move away. 'We'll take an easy trail along the riverside,' he promised.

Glowing with more than the kiss of the keen air against her cheeks, she followed him along the well-beaten trail, trying to remember all he had said. He looked entirely different out here on the snowfields with his peaked ski-cap pulled down over his eyes—a man of the mountains, utterly free and uncomplicated, a man attuned to nature who would have little time for subterfuge, a man to be trusted implicitly if the time ever came to confide in him. She had told him all she knew about Alice Silton, she reflected, and he had responded in the only way he could, with a polite interest in the problem of a passing stranger.

That was all she really was to him, she decided, so why should her pulses race when he came close or looked at her in that enigmatic way which seemed to doubt her?

'We'll go as far as the glacier,' he decided. 'It's an easy run for a beginner, since we have no nursery slopes up here.'

Enthralled by the fascination of the mountains, her initial fear was passing, driven out by the thrill of planing down the easier slopes in his wake with the ice-cold air catching at her breath and the sun warm on her cheeks. It was a stimulating adventure with Stephen there to guide her, in a world that was entirely their own without another being in sight. When she stumbled he was there, close behind her, to catch her before she fell and set her on her skis again, and soon she was able to laugh freely, joyfully, at this amazing new experience which was surely unique in all the world. Gaining confidence by the minute, she turned on his instruction to take the gentle trail back to the *schloss.* The sun, which had gone down rapidly, had lost its warmth, although the sky above their heads was still blue and clear, and suddenly the way back seemed an anticlimax.

'I've loved every minute!' she sighed. 'And now I've got the fever, I mean to persevere if ever I get the chance again. It's the most invigorating thing. No wonder Sophia is so keen.'

'She's quite an expert,' he admitted. 'She's been at it all her life, of course, and that's the easy way to learn. She was probably able to ski almost as soon as she could walk, and her burning ambition at one time was to be an instructress, but her mother nipped that in the bud, insisting she went to college instead.'

'Your aunt is a very strong-willed person,' she suggested. 'I wouldn't like to cross her.'

'Nobody does.'

'Except you?' She stole a look at his strong profile as he moved beside her. 'I can imagine you crossing swords from time to time.'

'Only when it affects my mother's interests,' he returned. 'I can be as hard as flint on those occasions, because my mother is apt to take the line of least resistance. She's a dreamer—an artist—and standing up to the Anastasias of this world doesn't appeal to her. I won't allow her to give up more than she should, however, because she has done that too often in the past.'

Once again his mouth tightened into a hard line, although before they had reached the riverbank they were laughing again. Encouraged by her surprising progress, Janet dug her sticks hard into the snow, sending herself forward at a considerable pace on the ice-hard trail until her skis came against a hidden obstacle and she found herself skidding ignominiously to the foot of the slope. A natural sense of preservation made her sit down, and she completed her progress in that undignified position to the sound of Stephen's laughter as he brought up the rear.

'You beast!' she laughed. 'I'm soaked to the skin!'

'I told you those trousers weren't made to sledge on!' he grinned. 'Stay where you are and give me your hand.'

He helped her to her feet as their eyes met mirthfully, standing there while she clung to his hands, the outside world completely forgotten. The world, however, was there in the shape of Sophia, who had come rapidly down from the ridge above them and was fast approaching the riverbank.

'You must be mad!' she cried. 'You can't career around like

that if this is your first lesson. I'm surprised at you, Stephen,' she added pointedly, 'making it all seem so trivial.'

The venom in her voice was reflected in her dark face as she surveyed them almost contemptuously, and Janet felt as if the ice-cold wind which now came down from the mountains had suddenly touched her heart.

Stephen took Sophia's reprimand in his stride.

'No harm done,' he declared. 'Jan seems to be well padded in all the right places!'

'If she keeps falling about like that, she'll never learn,' Sophia grumbled, moving ahead of them along the well-scored track. 'You know not to stay out too late,' she added scathingly, 'otherwise you'll freeze!'

With a perfunctory wave of her sticks she skied on, taking the slope to the *schloss* with practised ease, while Janet laboured after her, trying to remember all that Stephen had demonstrated about going uphill.

'Don't give a thought to falling back,' he recommended. 'I'm here to catch you if you do.'

'I'll never get there!' Janet declared, her cheeks pink with the effort she had made, her eyes glowing at the thought of her first lesson in the snow. 'It's marvellous exercise, though, and I'm sure it has done me good.'

'Don't let Sophia put you off. Like most experts, she can be intolerant at times,' he said, pulling up outside the *schloss*. 'She is also a great organiser, wanting everybody to join her long treks into the mountains sometimes even before they are ready.'

'She must have been disappointed at your lack of interest this afternoon,' Janet suggested. 'You could have gone with her, I suppose.'

He stopped to unbuckle her skis.

'Sophie's treks can last for a week or more, especially when she sees the snow melting away from her down here in the valley,' he said. 'The end of winter is a very sad time for her, especially when she is faced with a spring holiday in London or Paris.'

'With her mother,' Janet reflected. 'They are so different in every way.'

'Absolutely.' He moved out of his own skis. 'I don't think Sophia is at all vindictive; it's just that she has this thing about skiing which my aunt could never understand.'

'What does she do all summer once she has returned from holiday?' Janet asked as he turned to the door with both pairs of skis on his shoulder.

'She works here at the *schloss*. She doesn't like it, but she has to do something until the first autumn snowfall, when she comes into her own. It's a plus for the *schloss* to have an experienced instructor on the staff for the younger guests, and we don't have many beginners up here. They prefer Kitzbühel with its lifts and *après-ski* facilities to cosy evening sing-songs around the fire and and early nights the rule rather than the exception. Annastasia puts the last meal of the day on at eight o'clock, by the way,' he added, holding open the heavy door for her to precede him into the hall. 'Don't be late!'

'I won't,' she promised. 'I'll thank Sophia for the use of her skis when I see her again.'

'No need,' he said. 'They're probably an old pair she never uses. Sophia spends all her available cash on the latest equipment, and no doubt they are already out of date as far as she is concerned.'

'All the same, I have to thank her—and you, too, Stephen, for a wonderful experience,' she added. 'I've enjoyed myself so much.'

The inner hall was full of people, some of them newly returned from a final trek on the high snowfields, and Sophia stood among them, listening eagerly to their individual experiences and the times they had established along specific trails. Janet knew that it was all beyond her, but the spell of those high places seemed to fill the hall as they greeted

Stephen and included him in their conversation. I'm on the outside, looking in, she thought, although Stephen made a point of introducing her to most of the people he knew. There were an elderly couple from Munich and two Italians from Milan, plus an enthusiast from Vienna who had injured his leg.

'It is nothing,' he said in excellent English. 'Stephen, you should have been in medicine, you have such an interest in anyone who is hurt! But this is just a small sprain of the ankle which will not trouble me very much since I go home tomorrow.'

Sophia came to stand beside him.

'Make sure you see to it, Sigmund,' she admonished. 'You must be quite fit for the autumn, you know.'

'I'm thinking that my skiing days are coming to an end,' he sighed. 'Do you know that I will be sixty years old next weekend?'

'That's nothing!' Sophia declared from the distance of twenty summers. 'Carlo Bellini is much older, almost archaic, in fact, and he still comes up here every winter.'

'I know he does, and he'll probably die in the snow, which couldn't please him more, but I am a man who is fond of his creature comforts, my dear, so I shy from arthritis in my old age. I'm beginning to care about getting soaked to the skin and sleeping in isolated ski-huts in a blizzard. I'm concentrating more on warmth and a stimulating glass of schnapps at the end of the day.'

'You don't really mean that,' Sophia told him. 'You're just peeved about spraining your ankle on an easy run! It has injured your dignity more than your leg,' she suggested, putting her arm through his as he moved towards the stairs. 'Let me help you,' she offered. 'I believe your ankle *is* beginning to swell.'

Stephen followed them to the foot of the staircase.

'I'll take a look at it,' he offered, 'and then we can decide whether to send for a doctor or not.'

Sophia drew back, allowing him to take her place as Janet seized the opportunity to thank her.

'I used your skis this afternoon, Sophia,' she began. 'Stephen said you wouldn't mind because they were an old pair, but I want to thank you, all the same.'

Her smile was met by a dark frown.

'But I do mind,' Sophia declared. 'Unless you ask me beforehand. You could have broken those skis the way you were demonstrating for Stephen's benefit. Larking about, I suppose you would call it. Well, if you really want to learn to ski, that isn't the way to do it and—and Stephen should have more sense!' she concluded.

Angry and defiant, she was about to turn away when Janet said, 'I do appreciate that and I would like to learn, but I suppose I haven't the time. I won't be here long enough even for another lesson.'

Sophia's eyes narrowed.

'How long *are* you going to stay?' she demanded. 'We'll be closing the *schloss* to—visitors at the end of the month, although I believe the Baroness will be back from Salzburg by then.'

Stephen's mother, Janet thought. Of course, she would want her home to herself, if only for a week or two till her summer guests arrived, and perhaps that would mean that Stephen would be staying on with her.

CHAPTER FOUR

THEY dined in the long, raftered room facing the mountains, its dark oak refectory table set with the heavy silver which must have belonged to Von Erlachs long ago, and Janet couldn't help feeling sorry for Anastasia, who had prepared all the elaborate dishes which Sophia helped to carry in. Anastasia was virtually a servant in her old home, and she must be remembering the days when she had sat down at that same highly polished board to be served instead of serving. She saw the reflection of all these thoughts in Anastasia's dark face as their eyes met across the room, but Anastasia looked also at her daughter, dressed in a colourful dirndl skirt and fine white blouse, who seemed to hover behind Stephen as their most important guest.

Sophia waited on them without comment, as if it was the most natural thing for her to do, but her watchful eyes were on Stephen most of the time. She really is in love with him, Janet thought, but surely she must know about the elegant older woman he had embraced so affectionately at the entrance to the Goldener Hirsch?

Did Anastasia also know, and was that the reason for her resentment? If Stephen finally married her daughter, whom she could obviously manipulate with a little subtlety, wouldn't she find her own authority at the *schloss* greatly increased? It had taken years of insecurity and frustration to carve the deep lines of determination on Anastasia's face, and behind the dark eyes lay the bitterness of an old woman ready to stoop to any subterfuge to reclaim her power.

As far as Sophia was concerned it was probably quite natural that she should have fallen under her cousin's undoubted spell, drawn by the mesmeric quality about him which Janet herself had recognised on more than one occasion, but he was older—much older in Sophia's case, although he was a dependable male, a man unlikely to let her down in an uncomfortable situation, a man of amazing authority who could also be kind.

Looking quickly away from his smiling, suntanned face, she met Anastasia's calculating gaze across the table, realising that she had made an enemy through no fault of her own. Anastasia did not want her at the *schloss*, even as a guest, and it would not be long before she told her so.

Would Stephen protest, she wondered, or didn't it matter at all to him so long as the surface calm of the Schloss Erlach was not disturbed and they were seen to live in comparative harmony?

Even as they laughed and talked together with the remaining guests before the roaring log fire in the hall, it had the feeling of the calm before a storm. Sophia came to sit down at Stephen's feet, stirring a reluctant log until it burst into flame to send a shower of leaping yellow sparks up the wide chimney, while Wolfgang, who had also waited on them during the meal, sat in the shadows, looking on. When Janet spoke to him, she was surprised at the fluency of his English, until he told her that he had been educated in England, which left her wondering how he had ended up here at the *schloss* as Anastasia's willing slave.

An uneasy household, she reflected, looking round the circle of firelit faces as the grandfather clock in the corner struck twelve.

'Like Cinderella, I must depart!' she told Stephen. 'Do you really mean to take me with you in the morning?'

'Uttendorf is on my way,' he said.

'What's this about Uttendorf?' Sophia asked, turning from the fire. 'Why are you going there, Stephen?'

'It's Jan who is going,' he answered briefly. 'I'm on my way back to Salzburg.'

'Take me with you,' Sophia begged. 'There's nothing really exciting to do here now that the snow has almost gone.'

Janet found herself waiting for Stephen's answer with an odd feeling of loss in her heart. He had offered to take her as far as Uttendorf on his way to Salzburg and—foolishy, perhaps—she had been looking forward to the companionship they had shared so unexpectedly that afternoon on the ski-trail above the *schloss*, but it would be quite different if Sophia had her way.

'What about your mother?' he asked. 'She must need your help, even though she has so few guests left.'

'Oh, Mama won't mind,' Sophia declared confidently. 'She'll manage with Wolf to help her. You are coming back tomorrow?' she asked as an afterthought.

'That was the general idea,' Stephen agreed, 'but I have to warn you about Salzburg. You will be alone there for most of the day. I have two business meetings, and you know how dull they are.'

'Will you meet the Baroness?' Sophia asked. 'You generally do.'

'Only for a quick meal this time,' he said. 'She has a consultation with her doctor at the Carlton at three o'clock, and I hope to be on my way back by four.'

'That will suit me fine,' Sophia assured him. 'What time do you want to leave in the morning?'

'Eight o'clock.' For the first time Stephen looked across the hearth at Janet. 'Can you be ready by then?' he asked.

'I—yes, I'll be ready,' was all she could think of to say.

'I've half a notion Mama will be glad to be rid of me for a whole day!' Sophia laughed. 'What do you think, Wolf?' she demanded, turning to her mother's moody retainer, who still lurked by the dying fire.

Wolfgang lumbered to his feet, the deep colour of embarrassment staining his sallow cheeks.

'We do not need your help,' he said, 'since you are so unwilling to give it. I can see to everything your mother needs. She will not miss you.'

'So you say!' Sophia tossed her head. 'But you are slow, Wolf, and not at all imaginative. Sometimes I wonder why we put up with you at all.'

Janet moved towards the stairs, turning away from the scene of their disagreement. They were like a quarrelsome brother and sister bent on inflicting hurt on one another for a reason they did not understand. In their own individual ways they were both attached to Anastasia, willing enough to do her bidding but not to acknowledge the other as an equal. All the cruelty in Sophia's nature found its target in the lack-lustre servant favoured by her mother, while Wolf reacted with a jealousy which was only half hidden behind the mask of moodiness that had become the hallmark of his nature by now. Darkly handsome, he could have been attractive in his own right if it hadn't been for that perpetual scowl which effectively deadened his face, and once again she found herself thinking that Anastasia's household was indeed an uneasy one.

Rising early the following morning, she went down the wide staircase to find Anastasia alone in the dining-room where she was setting out cups and saucers on a side-table. An antique samovar bubbled pleasantly beside her for those of her guests who might prefer tea to coffee, filling the air with a faint smell of charcoal, while several large covered entrée dishes waited for them on the sideboard to make their choice of the substantial breakfast she had prepared. She glanced through the open door as Janet went in.

'You are alone,' she remarked. 'Are you still going to Salzburg?'

'I'm going as far as Uttendorf,' Janet explained. 'Stephen very kindly offered to take me.'

Anastasia returned her attention to the samovar, where the water was already boiling.

'Do you hope to come back with him?' she enquired.

'I—yes, that's what we intended. I understood you could put me up for a few days, since the *schloss* is so near to Uttendorf,' Janet pointed out.

'It is many miles distant,' Anastasia told her, 'and we will soon be closed. Already we have only a few guests left. Why are you going to Uttendorf?'

The abrupt question was so wholly unexpected that Janet could only answer her truthfully.

'To look for someone. I—that is why I came here with Stephen.'

'You met on a train. You have not known him for more than a few days,' the older woman remarked. 'Why should he bring you here?'

'I really don't know.' Janet had collected her wits at last. 'I think he was just being helpful to someone who was visiting Austria for the first time and didn't know her way about. He was being gallant, if you like, and I had no objection to that.'

Anastasia removed the lid from one of the entrée dishes.

'If you find this person you are looking for in Uttendorf will you stay there?' she asked.

'I don't think so.' Janet tried to explain. 'It's really information I'm looking for, not anyone specific, and I don't think I will find—the person I want to trace quite as easily as that.'

'But if you do, you will not be returning here.' Anastasia allowed the lid to clatter back on to the silver dish. 'We will not be displeased if you do not return,' she added firmly.

'I still have to come back for my luggage,' Janet pointed out equally firmly, 'so I'll be staying for another night, at least.'

Footsteps sounded across the uncarpeted hall, and suddenly Stephen was in the doorway.

'It will be just as you please,' Anastasia agreed. 'After all, we are an hotel.'

'What was all that about?' Stephen demanded, sitting down beside her at the round table by the window. 'You looked disconcerted when I appeared.'

'It had nothing to do with your coming down to breakfast,' Janet said, offering a smile. 'It was just that your aunt feels I may outstay my welcome here. I think she wants to empty the *schloss* as quickly as possible, and I suppose we can't blame her after a busy winter.'

An angry flush spread under his tan, although he said casually enough, 'My aunt has planned her holiday for the beginning of May, which is still two weeks away,' he said, 'so you are welcome to stay for as long as you like. If she has plans to empty the *schloss* earlier than that, they can easily be reversed and probably will be if my mother comes home.'

'In that case,' Janet offered, 'I would leave right away.'

He rose to investigate the contents of the entrée dishes.

'One step at a time,' he advised with his back turned. 'You have yet to make your enquiries in Uttendorf.'

Sophia came in, dressed for the journey to Salzburg in a red fur-trimmed coat and white knee-length boots, with a jaunty white fur hat on her head.

'You look like Father Christmas!' Stephen teased.

'Mother Christmas,' Sophia corrected him, 'since I've left my beard behind! You like me in red, Stevie—or so you once said!'

He made a place for her at the table, assuming she had not yet eaten.

'I've had a good breakfast already,' she told him. 'In the kitchen, which probably befits my status and gives Mama the opportunity to insist that I should help with the cooking.'

'She was also willing to give you the day off,' Stephen reminded her. 'Is Wolf coming with us to Salzburg?'

'Wolf? Of course not!' Sophia dismissed Wolf without a second thought. 'He will have to stay, since I won't be back before dinner.'

'I'll bring the car round,' Stephen said, pushing back his chair. 'When you are ready, we'll get on our way.'

'I'm ready now,' Sophia pointed out. 'It's only Jan who is holding us back.'

Janet gulped her coffee, rising swiftly to her feet.

'I won't be more than five minutes,' she promised, making for the door.

In those few minutes, however, Sophia had completed her plan, and when Janet followed her outside she was already seated in the front of the car, leaving their unexpected guest to travel in state in the back seat.

Anastasia appeared at the door to see them off, unable to suppress a smile of satisfaction when she saw the seating arrangements.

'Remember what I told you about Salzburg,' she said. 'Keep close to Stephen and don't go window-shopping as you usally do and forget the time.'

Sophia shrugged, refusing to make any promises as she settled back in the seat she had been so determined to secure.

Janet contented herself with the magnificent view unfolding all around her on the journey to Uttendorf. Every valley boasted its small village with an onion-domed church as its centre and a river flowing down from the high snowfields, while spectacular mountains rose majestically on the horizon, and the sun glittered on their summits to make small haloes of light along their pristine flanks. For a moment it seemed that they were travelling through a lost world where nothing moved but the car, speeding along the narrow road which might take her to a final rendezvous with Alice Silton.

But what if Alice was dead or gone off to the other side of the world with the man she had married when her hope of ever seeing Richard again had faded? She was working on such flimsy clue that it seemed impossible that she should suddenly come face to face with Alice, but ever since she had arrived in Austria some instinct had told her that the woman she sought was not far away.

Wishful thinking? She supposed it was because she wanted Richard to find eventual happiness with the girl he had never stopped loving since they had parted so foolishly all those years ago.

They came at last to her destination, where Stephen pulled up in front of a busy tavern in the centre of the town.

'We've time for a coffee,' he decided, rubbing his hands together as he got out of the car. 'Then Uttendorf is yours to explore where you wish.'

If it hadn't been for Sophia's presence, Janet might have asked for his help, but Sophia seemed disinclined to linger in the small town she apparently knew so well when she had Salzburg in her sights.

'There's nothing here,' she decided, 'except perhaps if you go on to Zell and Saalbach. Do you remember, Stevie, when we were caught up there by the avalanche and everybody thought we were gone for good? It was a marvellous time!' she exulted. 'Stevie,' she insisted, 'you do not say that you remember, but I know you do!'

'I remember how foolish we were,' he told her, 'going on when we should have turned back.'

'I would never have turned back,' Sophia declared 'and neither would you! Because you would never have allowed me to call you chicken-livered,' she laughed. 'That was what you feared more than the avalanche!'

He smiled at the accusation, not contradicting her as he led the way into the warm little tavern where mulled wine and coffee were being served round a huge wood stove in the centre of the room.

Sophia refused to sit down, warming her hands on the mug of coffee when it was brought to her.

'I can't think what you want to do here,' she said to Janet, 'But it must be something special when you don't want to come to Salzburg with us.'

'Jan has explained all that,' Stephen said. 'She has already made her enquiries in Salzburg.'

'And drawn a blank?' Sophia glanced from one of them to the other. 'What are you hiding?' she demanded. 'You sound almost guilty, the way you try to avoid an explanation.'

'Janet will tell you that there is nothing to avoid,' Stephen returned as he put down his empty glass. 'She is here to make some enquiries, as she said, but that is all.'

Sophia moved towards the door.

'Then let's get on', she suggested. 'You said you had to be in Salzburg before twelve.'

She was already at the door when Stephen turned to Janet.

'Good luck,' he said evasively. 'Perhaps you will need it.'

'What time shall we meet?' she asked. 'And where?'

'Here will be as good a place as any,' he decided. 'Then you needn't stand around in the cold. It's central, too, and easy to find if you walk around. Shall we say seven o'clock?'

She nodded, watching them go, Stephen striding out behind his cousin with most eyes turned on him as he closed the door firmly behind him.

A waiter came to bring her more coffee, while she pulled the snapshot of Alice Silton from her wallet.

'Do you know this person?' she asked. 'Maybe you have seen her?'

Struggling with her English, the young man shook his head.

'Not so good,' he decided, handing back the fading picture. 'You try elsewhere.'

She felt disappointed, but this was no more than a start, and by keeping her mind firmly fixed on her reason for being here in the first place she might be able to forget Sophia, or Stephen, for that matter. By now he would be half-way to Salzburg to see his ladyfriend, no doubt. Or perhaps she was even his fiancée, although she had seemed older than he was in that brief glimpse she had had of them in front of the Goldener

Hirsch. Remembering how he had dismissed the age-gap between his mother and the Baron, she supposed that would not worry him too much, and it should not concern her, she decided crossly, since it was none of her business.

Or was it? Was she allowing Stephen Kempson to dominate her life, even to creep into her heart?

Virgorously rejecting the idea, she told herself she had work to do, but even though she contacted the police and called in at shop after likely shop, again and again she drew a blank. By six o'clock it seemed as if Alice Silton had never existed, and she returned to the town centre to wait for Stephen.

People were hurrying to and fro, bent on their various pursuits, all of them warmly wrapped up against the increasing cold, none of them giving her more than a perfunctory glance, and suddenly, devastatingly, she felt alone. She had come here in search of a will-o-the-wisp, and even Stephen seemed unwilling to help her, yet how could she possibly expect his co-operation when they were little more than strangers even now?

Remembering how he had come to Gray's Inn in search of Richard, she found herself wondering what his business could have been, the business he had refused to discuss with her or even Nigel, who might have been able to advise him.

Dismissing his reason, she could only think of the strangeness of their subsequent meeting on the train and the fact that he had told her very little about himself, while she had spilled out most of the details about herself, even the more sensitive ones like her reason for wanting to help Richard as much as she could because she had depended upon him for so long.

She looked up at the surrounding mountains to find them staring coldly back at her in the half-dusk as clouds began to gather behind them, taking away some of the magic from the little town which seemed to have turned its back on her.

A horse-drawn sleigh rattled past, its bells jangling as the horses tossed their heads, but there seemed to be nothing else to see. Nevertheless, she had the renewed strong feeling that, near at hand, there was some clue to Alice Silton's whereabouts among those strange, encircling mountains, or even back in Salzburg where Sebastian and Hans Dietrich had failed to tell her the absolute truth. She would go back there, she decided, and try again.

Waiting for the car's return in the tavern where they had parted company, she watched the light fade and the first star come out to pierce the sky. It was a beautiful place, this Tyrol of Stephen's, a place where she could have lived contentedly for the rest of her life.

When he came, he did not seem to be greatly surprised by her failure.

'I feel I should go back to Salzburg,' she confessed. 'Perhaps I left the Goldener Hirsch too quickly.'

'If I influenced you, I'm sorry,' he apologised, 'but Salzburg isn't too far away. I can't help you,' he added unfeelingly, 'unless you can be absolutely sure of your true motive for coming to Austria.'

The criticism hurt.

'You doubt my word!' she exclaimed. 'You suspect me of lying to you all this time?'

'Not exactly.' He led her into the shadows away from the hanging lamps above the stove. 'I know your credentials are intact because I verified them in London before you came here.'

She looked at him aghast.

'Then—you *were* following me when we left Victoria?' she accused him.

'Checking up on you,' he agreed. 'I had to be quite sure why exactly you were coming to Austria.'

'Stephen, who are you?' she demanded, her pulses racing. 'You're not—a private eye?'

He laughed at the suggestion.

'Not professionally,' he said, 'but I do admit I have an axe to grind. I needed to know why you were making this journey for Richard Cosgrave and why he didn't come himself.'

'I told you why,' she protested. 'I didn't lie about that. I said Richard wanted to find Alice Silton and I was helping him.'

'Why?' he asked, a hardness in his eyes she had seen there before.

'Because I owe him so much—because we have been friends for so long. He is my legal guardian as well as my godfather, and when he asked me to do this for him I couldn't refuse.' She drew a deep breath. 'It's proving harder than I thought to trace Alice,' she confessed, 'but I will some day!'

'And pay back all your debts to Richard,' he suggested.

'I could never do that! You can't hope to repay years and years of love and protection just by helping out in an emergency.'

It was true, she thought. She would never be able to do enough for her godfather for giving her a home at Beeston, where she had known so much happiness in the past. Every year she had gone there in the summer with her widowed mother to spend an idyllic month at the rambling old house by the river where they swam and punted and walked on the towpath, and talked about the future when she would be grown up and able to help the lonely widow who had worked so hard for her ever since her father had been killed in an accident. Beeston had always been a precious place for them both, and when her mother had died that winter so unexpectedly and Richard had offered her a home there, she could harldy believe how fortunate she was. To go back to Beeston from time to time, to look on it as her home, had meant more to her than anyone could imagine. More than she could even hint about to this remote stranger who had shown her some of the same kindness for a reason best known to himself when he had found her accommodation at the *schloss*.

'Lady,' he said grimly, 'you will have to do better than that.' He took hold of her arm, his fingers gripping like steel as he held her gaze in a compelling stare. 'I know you're involved,' he said, 'and I mean to find out just how deeply.'

He had changed completely. He was no longer the aloof, disinterested man on the train, but a man determined to exact the truth from someone he had suspected of duplicity all along.

'Why?' she asked, her voice none too steady as she looked back into those relentless eyes.

'Because,' he said, 'I believe you are looking for my mother.'

The revelation stunned her into silence as he continued to hold her, and she could only look at him incredulously, wondering if she had heard aright.

'Your mother?' she repeated, aghast. 'But—the Baroness?'

He led her further into the shadows to a table under one of the high windows where they were less likely to be overheard, explaining curtly, 'Alice Silton married my father in Paris where he worked at the Embassy, and after I was born they moved to Munich where my father died. I was under a year old at the time, so there was no way she could go out to work, and no possibility of continuing her career in opera until I was older. Apparently there was very little money left for her to live on, but she was determined to try. She sang in bars and riverside cafés because she had no other choice.' Suddenly his jaw tightened. 'That's why I am determined to protect her now that I can.'

'She—never returned to England?' Janet's voice was still rough with shock. 'She never went home?'

'Home at that time was Munich. She had made friends there who helped her when they could, and there was no reason for her to return.' He paused, gazing down at the table as if he could see much of the past mirrored on its polished surface. 'Several years later she met Ludwig Von Erlach who had been a friend of my father in Paris and he offered her a job. He was busy on his final concerto and he was going blind. He needed someone to work with him who understood music, and in exchange he helped her with her career as a singer. She never quite made the heights in opera she had aspired to in England, but she gained a reputation as a reliable performer under his direction and she was grateful.'

'Grateful enough for her to marry him.' Janet sat down on the edge of a chair. 'It must have been difficult for her, bringing up a child in those circumstances in a foreign country.'

'She had accepted it as her own. It seemed that the Baron needed her, although there was a gap of twenty-odd years in their ages. He was determined to finish his concerto and she was the person who could help him. His wife had died many years before they met, so they had a shared experience in that respect. Music was the thing that drew them together until, finally, they married.'

'And you, Stephen?' she asked quietly.

'I was sent to England to be educated when I was ten,' he explained. 'It must have been a sacrifice as far as my mother was concerned, but she was determined to do it for my sake. It was before she married the Baron and money must have been very tight, but she managed. I spent all my holidays at the *schloss*, loving every minute, although I considered England my real home. I think that was what she wanted. Ludwig was now very frail, but he directed my career and my mother had grown fond of him, I suppose. When he asked her to marry him I was already established in Paris with the firm I work for now—an English firm, by the way—and I returned to the *schloss* from time to time to see them both. The Baron was a wonderful man, dedicated to his music, and he offered my mother the freedom she needed to pursue her career if she wanted to, but he had already given her so much in affectionate understanding that she was there by his side till he died.'

A rush of compassion filled Janet's heart.

'Thank you for telling me,' she said. 'It helps me to understand.'

His face darkened, remembering the more recent past.

'There are a few other things to clear up,' he said, 'and Sophia is waiting in the car.'

Janet had forgotten about Sophia.

'Yes,' she said, moving towards the door. 'Did she enjoy her day in Salzburg?'

'I fear so! She spent most of it going round the shopping arcades in search of a summer wardrobe.'

He had tried to speak lightly, but she sensed the reserve in him which had first made him suspicious of her intentions.

'If we could talk . . .' she suggested as they reached the door. 'Perhaps when we get back to the *schloss*? At the moment I can't think what to do.'

'You could return to London,' he suggested unemotionally.

'Yes.' They stood in the doorway with Sophia looking across the pavement at them. 'Perhaps that would be the best idea.'

But what to tell Richard when she got there? That she had found Alice but hadn't been able to talk to her because her son, Stephen, was determined that she should stay in Austria where he thought she belonged?

'Get into the car,' he ordered. 'We have quite a lot to talk about.'

Turning round from the front passenger seat, Sophia studied her with interest.

'If I didn't totally disbelieve in them, I'd say you had seen a ghost,' she reflected. 'What has happened to make you look so scared, Janet?'

'Nothing. Nothing at all,' Janet protested. 'Perhaps I'm just feeling—cold.'

Had she seen the ghost of an old love-affair stealing away into the shadows of a dark little tavern in the centre of a Tyrolean town, she wondered, or was it just that love as Richard and Alice had once known it was dead? It couldn't be!

Richard had sent her half-way across a continent to find his lost love, and she couldn't give up as easily as that. She had to question Stephen to know what he thought, and what Alice Silton thought now that she was the Baroness Von Erlach and lived in a *schloss.*

The moon appeared over the mountains, sending dark shadows ahead of them as they drove on, and everywhere she looked there were more shadows, dark under the pines, grey where the snow had drifted beneath a bank. In this fantasy world of light and shade nothing stood out clearly, so that it all seemed a reflection of her own thoughts, confusing her the more.

Silence reigned in the big, comfortable car, deepening the sense of foreboding which she felt, as if Stephen had virtually taken her prisoner and would not release her until he was sure of her innocence. Yet, what did he consider she had done? She had told him quite frankly from the beginning why she had come to Austria, hiding nothing, yet his manner remained guarded, even suspicious now that she knew who his mother really was. It was only natural that he should want to shield the Baroness's privacy, of course, but how could he blame her for pleading Richard's cause now that she had explained her reason?

When they reached the foot of the valley they could see the Schloss Erlach just ahead of them, picked out against the snow because most of the lights were on and twinkling as brightly as the myriad stars in the sky above, seeming to welcome them home.

Which wasn't strictly true, Janet thought instantly. The lights might be shining out for Stephen and Sophia, but not for her. If they had been, she realised, her heart would have risen like a bird to soar above them till it reached the distant stars.

'It's good to be home,' Sophia declared, leaning forward in her seat to admire a vista she must have known by heart for many years. 'It is always the same every time I go away. You must feel it, too, Stephen,' she added. 'You must be happy to be back!'

He swung the car up under the retaining wall where the shadows were deepest.

'After a day in Salzburg,' he said lightly, 'anybody would be happy to be back. Are you still cold, Jan,' he added, 'or has the journey warmed you up?' He leaned back in his seat, turning his head to look at her as he switched on the interior light above her head. 'I hope the long day hasn't tired you too much.'

'It hasn't tired me as much as it has defeated me,' she admitted as Sophia got out to collect her day's shopping from the boot, 'but I'll get over that, I dare say, when I have had time to think clearly again. Perhaps I shouldn't have asked your help, Stephen—I wouldn't have done if I had known the truth—but it seemed reasonable at the time. I had no idea you would resent it so much.'

Sophia came back to tap on the closed window.

'I need help,' she announced. 'Are you two going to sit there for the rest of the night?'

'Let me take some of your parcels,' Janet offered, getting out.

'Stephen will do it!' Sophia looked challengingly at her cousin on the far side of the car. 'He was the one who thought I had bought too much!'

Janet went on into the *schloss*, where most of the remaining guests were gathered in the hall.

'You have had a nice day, I hope?' Carlo Bellini asked, jumping to his feet to help Sophia with the few parcels she had carried in. 'You look overloaded!'

'It's nothing to what Stephen looks like!' Sophia laughed. 'He's right behind me!'

'I cannot imagine Stephen shopping in bulk,' Carlo smiled. 'And you, Miss Blair,' he added, turning to where Janet stood in the background, 'surely you have something other than your purse to show us on your return?'

'Janet didn't go to Salzburg,' Sophia told him with a trace of satisfaction in her high-pitched voice. 'She went only to Uttendorf, where she spent the day looking for someone.'

'And were you successful in your search?' Carlo enquired, making room for Janet at the fire.

'Yes—and no,' she admitted, wondering if Stephen saw her confusion as he put Sophia's parcels down on a side-table. 'I suppose you could say I was successful in one respect.'

'But not in another?' Carlo's wise old eyes twinkled. 'The saying is that half a fact is almost as good as the whole, if it leads you eventually to what you want to know.'

Sophia laughed.

'Carlo, you are full of odd little sayings!' she declared. '*Bons mots* that slew everyone when they first heard them, but how can only half a fact be important? What about the other half, which could easily cancel it out?'

'Ah, that can be explained,' he promised. 'When you have even the smallest amount of the truth, you are half-way to discovering it all!'

'You talk in riddles!' Sophia told him. 'Tonight I don't even begin to understand!'

Anastasia came out of the shadows to throw an extra log on the fire.

'You are early returned,' she remarked, taking note of Sophia's parcels with a jaundiced eye. 'What have you been spending all your money on?'

'Not quite all of it,' her daughter assured her. 'I brought one of the new ski-suits and a dress, which will please you, I'm sure.'

'What need have you of another ski-suit at the end of the season?' her mother demanded. 'The ones you have are well enough to be going on with.'

Sophia's glance slid to where Stephen stood at the other side of the fireplace.

'The old ones are now out of fashion,' she declared. 'Everything is one-piece nowadays for comfort and reliability,' she added to refute all argument.

For once Anastasia was not disposed to argue.

'It is your own money you are wasting,' she pointed out with a logic not always in evidence, 'but don't come to me for help when we reach London, remember. You have an allowance which I consider adequate, and you also earn a reasonable wage while you are here.'

Evidently Sophia was paid for her services at the *schloss*, but the fact rankled.

'I could earn much more if I worked elsewhere,' she pointed out sullenly. 'You don't even pay Wolf a decent wage.'

'He has not yet complained,' said Anastasia. 'He is obviously content.'

'I don't think he always will be,' Sophia argued, 'and he hates London as much as I do. One of these days neither of us will go with you,' she predicted.

A dark colour rose under her mother's sallow skin.

'While you are dependent on me, you will do as I ask,' she said. 'Wolf is aware of this and you must be also. But we will talk of London some other time,' she added dismissively, 'when we are ready to leave here.'

'Stephen,' Sophia asked, 'have you made up your mind about coming to London with us? It would be much more fun.'

Her cousin paused on his way to the door.

'I may even do that,' he said, 'Since I have a few things to clear up there.'

'And then you will return to Paris?' Sophia looked eager. 'We will also go to Paris on our way back from London.'

'I work in Paris, remember,' he said. 'Of course I will be there when you return.'

Anastasia stooped towards the fire, stirring the logs into a fiercer blaze whose orange light was suddenly reflected in her eyes.

'When do you expect your mother to return here?' she asked, looking across the hearth at Stephen. 'It is necessary for me to know before I can make my final preparations to go to London.'

Stephen considered the point.

'In about a week's time, I would say. She believes in the cure at the Carlton and it appears to have done her good. The rest has helped, anyway.'

Standing between them on her way to the door, Janet was acutely aware of conflict, a fire in both their eyes which suggested antagonism and a determination to win. It was a conflict which ran deep and which had probably existed for a long time, she decided, even although she was already conscious of Anastasia's desire to see Stephen and Sophia married one day, which would put her daughter very firmly in charge at the *schloss*.

So, what of Stephen? When she looked at him, Janet's heart seemed to miss a beat, although deep down she was aware of a guarded reserve in him which she might never be able to penetrate. He could be everything to a woman, courteous and kind and even tender, but if he felt betrayed he would be without mercy.

Wondering if that was too harsh a judgement, she walked through to the empty hallway, something forlorn stirring in her heart as she crossed the expanse of polished wood floor to mount the stairs. Less than a week ago he had come into her life, and now it seemed as if he had always been there.

CHAPTER FIVE

FOR the next two days Stephen seemed to be avoiding her, going off with Sophia to ski while Janet spent her time around the *schloss* trying to avoid Anastasia, whose main task seemed to be to speed her departing guests and close up their rooms for the duration of the holiday she was determined to take.

There was no more talk of the Baroness once she had discovered that Stephen's mother would return to take over in her absence, but she appeared to be working her aggression out on the *schloss* itself. Windows were thrown open to the early morning sun and mattresses aired from their ledges, while duvets and bedlinen were washed, dried and stored away in the big oak cupboards along the walls. The little *schloss* hummed with activity after each departure, and when there were only Carlo and his friend left, Janet began to feel that she had outstayed her welcome. Yet, something kept her there, something stronger even than the need to find Alice Silton, who was now the Baroness Von Erlach.

Stephen and his cousin always returned from the piste before the sun went down. The night air still had a chill on its breath, which even the bright warmth of midday could not conquer, and contentment seemed to wrap round them as they relaxed before the wood fire afterwards to re-live their day's activities on the high snowfields. Sophia came in glowing with her activity, her cheeks like bright red apples, her eyes sparkling as she warmed her hands at the fire. As far as Stephen was concerned, the hard sorties into the mountains apparently helped to clear his mind as much as working off surplus energy, although once or twice Janet saw the dark frown between his brows again and the old tension around his mouth.

When Sophia went reluctantly to help her mother in the kitchen, Janet seized her opportunity to speak to him privately, feeling that she was presenting him with a challenge.

'Stephen,' she asked abruptly, 'where can I find the Baroness?'

He was standing beside the long window which commanded the view across the valley to the snow-capped mountains, and she had come up behind him without him appearing to notice. It took him a full minute to turn round and answer her.

'All in good time,' he said briefly. 'When she hears the truth, she may not want to see you.'

'Which means you haven't told her who I am?'

'No.'

'Or why I am here.' It was a statement rather than a question. 'But, Stephen, it's all so simple,' she protested. 'Richard only wants to meet her again.'

He took a step towards her in the fading light.

'To make amends?' His voice was harsh. 'How does he think he'll do that? He jilted her a long time ago, and it took her many years to forget him. She was happy with my father, even in love with him in a way, but sometimes I wonder if she ever put that first love-affair completely behind her.'

'And I'm sure Richard never did!' she cried. 'In all these years he never married.'

'Is that the criterion?' he asked coldly.

'When you marry,' she said, 'perhaps you will understand what I mean.' In spite of herself, a note of pleading softened her voice. 'Especially if you marry the right person.'

He looked down at her for a moment, almost as if he wanted to believe her, until the hardness darkened his eyes again.

'I have no plans to marry,' he said. 'Not until I am absolutely certain of my mother's future. For a long time she has been receiving mysterious phone calls threatening her person if she does not leave the *schloss* and return to England, and they have played havoc with her nerves. It is part of her reason for remaining at the Carlton, where all her calls are monitored, but even there the odd threat has filtered through. Some time ago,' he added deliberately, 'several of these calls were traced to London.'

She stood back, scarcely able to believe what she had just heard.

'You're accusing Richard!' she gasped. 'I can't believe it!' When her first amazement passed, she added slowly, 'Then you are also accusing me.'

He took her by the shoulders, almost shaking her.

'I must find out the truth,' he said. 'Surely you can see that? I have to be *sure*.'

For a moment she could not answer him, asking a question instead.

'Why do you think Richard would do such a thing?'

'You must ask yourself that question,' he returned bluntly. 'A long time has passed since that youthful affair, and he must have suspected that she had married.'

She returned his gaze with anger in his eyes.

'You're talking about revenge!' she accused him. 'Which means you can't understand how he feels. Once you are in love like that, you would never seek revenge, not even for infidelity.'

'You have a touching faith in your godfather,' he said, 'and I must admit it's not the sort of thing I would expect a well-known barrister to do, but there have been exceptions, you must admit.'

'He sent me to find her. Can't you understand that? He wants her back. Why would he try to frighten her in such a way?' she demanded. 'You're not making sense. He loves her—he has always loved her!'

He was still looking down at her, holding her as he searched her distressed face for something of the truth.

'At the moment,' he said, releasing her abruptly, 'I am more concerned with the threatening phone calls. Someone wants my mother to quit the Schloss Erlach and I mean to find out who—and why.'

She took a step towards him.

'Then—let me help you,' she offered.

Instantly he drew back.

'I don't think so,' he decided. 'This is something I have to do for myself.'

His reaction had been so sure, so final, and she could not protest further. Carlo Bellini came to join them at the window.

'My holiday has come to an end,' he sighed. 'Why is it, Stephen, that we are so unwilling to leave this place?'

'Because we both live in capital cities, and this offers us the peace we need on occasion,' Stephen answered. 'Paris is the noisiest city I know, with the exception of Rome.'

'You must come to Milan,' Carlo declared. 'Night and day there is noise and distraction everywhere, but I tell myself that I am getting old when I notice it so much. I thought you young people appreciated it, though—something to do all the time with no chance of boredom creeping in to spoil the fun! What do you say, Janet?' he asked, turning enquiring eyes in her direction. 'Would you spend the rest of your life here, if you could?'

'Gladly!' Spontaneously she answered him, looking out over the pristine snow. 'But I have to work in London and I have to go back soon.'

'With regret, I am sure!' Unashamedly he looked beyond her to where Stephen stood listening to her confession.

'With regret,' she agreed. 'The Tyrol is so beautiful. I had no idea, except for the odd picture I have seen, and even they didn't convey its true magic.'

'It will draw you back again,' Carlo predicted. 'A single visit will never be enough, but now that you know about the Schloss Erlach you will not hesitate about a choice of hotels. I come every year, as do many others, and we have become like a big, happy family now, always choosing the same time of year—the coming of spring.'

The coming of spring! Janet turned away with the lovely phrase ringing in her ears, but so many springs would come and go in this silent valley, and she would never return.

During the meal which followed she was aware of Anastasia looking closely at her from the far side of the table as she served Carlo and his only other fellow-guest, who would probably leave with him in the morning. It would be a source of irritation to have only one remaining guest to contend with, and Janet was not greatly surprised when she broached the subject at her first opportunity.

After dinner they generally sat by the fire for an hour, joined by Sophia when her kitchen duties were completed, but Carlo excused himself at the dining-room door.

'I have possessions scattered around all over the place,' he admitted, 'and I must gather them together before I go to bed. Otherwise, I shall be in a panic in the morning, wondering where everything is.'

'Do you want the sleigh to take you to the village?' Stephen asked. 'Or I could easily run you to Kitzbühel to catch your train.'

'I am invited to go all the way in Luigi's car,' Carlo explained, 'which solves many of my problems because we live quite close together in Milan. It will be no inconvenience to him.'

Stephen went to put his own car away with Sophia in earnest pursuit.

'Would you take a look at one of my skis?' she asked. 'I thought it was going its own way yesterday!'

Janet remained for a few minutes by the fire, watching the logs subsiding in the iron basket as they finally burned away to a powdering of grey ash. There was a sadness about a dying fire which spelt defeat, she thought, the bright sparks from the logs no longer bounding joyously up the chimney to escape into the cold night air above. It was like waiting for the end of something, yet in the morning Wolf would come with fresh kindling in his basket to renew it but when she left the *schloss* the fire which leapt in her veins as she waited for Stephen's return would never be rekindled.

Anastasia came up behind her.

'Do you wish me to renew the fire?' she asked. 'Wolfgang is busy elsewhere. There is much work to do when we are preparing to close.'

'Oh—no, thank you,' Janet refused. Stephen and Sophia would not return until much later. 'I must go to bed.'

'How long do you mean to stay here?'

The question was so abrupt and so definitely aggressive that Janet paused on her way to the door.

'A day or two, perhaps,' she suggested tentatively.

'That is too long. Our only other guests will go tomorrow, and most of the rooms will be closed. The hall and dining-room take much heating, and when we are alone as a family we occupy smaller rooms at the back of the house.'

'I don't mind moving or making do,' Janet said, 'and I wouldn't expect to be waited on if it was an inconvenience, but I would like to stay till—till the weekend,' she decided hurriedly.

Anastasia stiffened.

'That will not be possible,' she said. 'Stephen had no right to bring you here in the first place when he knew our rules.'

'It was obliging of him.' Face to face with this gaunt, determined woman, Janet was suddenly equally determined. 'Stephen mentioned that you would not be going to London till May, so perhaps it won't matter so much if I stay for a day or two longer. I—have a great deal to sort out and I need a little time to think about it. I have to change my plans.'

That was true enough. She hadn't decided what to do about the Baroness who had once been Alice Silton, but she couldn't bring herself to tell Anastasia why she had come to Austria.

'Stephen has nothing to do with the running of the *schloss*,' Anastasia told her angrily. 'He is only here on holiday, like yourself.'

'The Baroness is his mother,' Janet felt compelled to remind her.

'Even she is not here by right!' The sheer venom in the older woman's tone took Janet completely by surprise. 'She is a Von Erlach only by marriage, and her son is nothing at all!'

'She was your brother's wife,' Janet pointed out, 'and she nursed him faithfully through his last illness.'

'And shut me out!' Anastasia cried. 'We were brother and sister, a closer tie than just husband and wife.'

'Surely you don't believe that, Frau Waldburger,' Janet protested.

'I believe justice should be done! I am no better than a servant here in my own home,' Anastasia declared. 'A good cook, a *hausfrau*, able to do all the menial tasks to the Baroness's satisfaction.'

Embarrassed by such an outburst, Janet could only suggest that she needed a change of scene.

'Perhaps you need a break,' she said. 'We all do at times. Will you take your holiday even if the Baroness doesn't come home?'

'I intend to,' Anastasia said. 'That is why I am asking you to leave quickly.'

She went out with a swish of her long black skirt, leaving her guest to contemplate the dead ash in the fireplace until the big raftered room began to turn cold.

Standing at her bedroom window before she finally drew the heavy velvet curtains between her and the silent night, Janet realised how reluctant she was to make a final decision. She had come to Austria to find out about Alice Silton, and now the answer was so near at hand that she could hardly believe her luck, but in the process she had involved Stephen or, more truthfully, he had invovled himself in his mother's defence, which was only natural. There had been no rule which had said she should fall in love with him in the process, but that was what had happened. Swiftly and unequivocally she had fallen in love with a man she had only known for the shortest time, a man who had entered her life without warning in the strangest possible way, a man unknown to her a couple of weeks ago, who could have been Richard's son. If Alice and Richard had married all those years ago in London, life for her might have been changed, but it would have been to her godfather's advantage. She felt sure about that, although she had never met the Baroness and perhaps never would.

On the snow-covered trail beneath the *schloss*, two figures came into view one carrying a pair of skis. Sophia and Stephen returning after trying the damaged ski out in the moonlight! They were both warmly wrapped up with snow-hoods over their heads, but she would have recognised Stephen's tall figure anywhere, and Sophie in her bright red suit was equally outstanding. They had gone off together in the moonlight, in spite of the biting cold and were returning together, hand in hand.

In spite of his teasing attitude towards his cousin, Stephen could be physically attracted to her and nothing would please Anastasia more. But what of his other love, the tall, elegantly dressed older woman he had kissed with such familiarity on the steps of the Goldener Hirsch? Was she someone he couldn't have, their love forbidden by the fact that she was already married?

Swiflty she drew the curtains across the window, plunging her room into darkness. Was that what happened when love went wrong, when there could be nothing left but agony and regret? It had happened to Richard long ago, just as it might be happening to Stephen now, and soon it would happen to her. One way or another she seemed destined to tread the same path as Alice Silton, and her heart grew heavy at the thought.

All the same, she decided instantly, I have to go on. I have to seek out the Baroness in Salzburg before I leave Austria for good.

She would be taking the news of Alison Silton's whereabouts back to Richard, at least, and that was why she had come.

The following morning she was first down for breakfast, beating even Sophia in her eagerness to get out into the snow. The day before she had seen Wolfgang working at the stables which occupied a separate block behind the *schloss*, and she went there to find him. In a green baize apron and incongruous-looking ski cap, he was brushing down two horses which drew the sleigh.

'Good morning, Wolf!' she greeted him. 'Are you going out with the sleigh?'

He turned to consider her, surprised that anyone should be around at such an early hour.

'I go each morning to collect milk and the newspapers,' he informed her respectfully. 'Why do you want to know?'

This was where she must tread carefully, Janet thought.

'Will you be going as far as Uttendorf?' she asked.

He shook his head.

'Not as far as that.'

'Well—anywhere near, where I could perhaps get a bus to Salzburg.' She had already decided not to ask Stephen for the help he would be unwilling to give. 'I have to go there rather urgently,' she added. 'Something has cropped up since yesterday.'

He considered her request and her reason for making it with a slow deliberation for which she could have shaken him.

'I'm not supposed to take anyone out without the mistress's permission.'

'You mean Frau Waldburger? But you are taking the sleigh out anyway,' she protested.

'It is not the same. The sleigh is a routine job.' He was studying her with interest now. 'Why do you want to go to

Salzburg so early in the morning? There's a car going that way later on with Signor Bellini and Signor Ovetti in it on their way back to Milan.'

'They may not leave till after lunch,' she argued, 'and I would like to be in Salzburg before then.'

He ran a practised hand over the nearest horse's flank.

'What you ask is impossible,' he told her. 'I have a tight schedule and, besides, I do not go as far as Uttendorf. Only to the village, and there you would not find a bus going out till after ten o'clock. It takes a round-about route and returns from Salzburg almost immediately.'

Janet was disappointed. There was nothing for it but to go back to the *schloss* defeated and be forced to ask Stephen for the help he might so easily refuse.

'What are you doing here?'

She had not seen Stephen in the doorway, although Wolfgang could have noticed him standing there.

'Stephen!' she exclaimed. 'I didn't expect you to be out so early.'

'Evidently not.' He moved aside to allow her through the doorway. 'You were asking Wolf for the use of the sleigh. May I ask why?'

She turned to face him in the brighter light outside the stable door.

'Because I have to go back to Salzburg, and I know you would not agree to take me there.' Determination showed in every line of her small, taut figure. 'You have no real reason for refusing me, Stephen. I can't do your mother any harm.'

He walked with her over the frozen snow.

'That may be true,' he agreed guardedly, 'but I have no intention of letting you rush in to confront her with Richard Cosgrave's amazing suggestion before I have had a chance to prepare her for the shock of hearing from him after so long.'

'I know it will be a shock.' She halted on the icy pathway to look at him. 'I acknowledge that, Stephen, but I can't go back to London without seeing her or—having some message from her to take back to Richard. He would never forgive me if I left this job half done, and I would never forgive myself.'

In the cold light of morning he looked inflexible.

'What do you expect her to say?' he asked.

'I think I want her to say that she will meet him, in London or Paris, if only to heal some of the hurt they have caused each other since they parted.'

'Your godfather was to blame for that,' he said, tight-lipped. 'I believe she wrote to him from Paris and he didn't answer.'

'How can that have happened?' She continued to search his face. 'Richard didn't mention a letter.'

'He could have forgotten or changed his mind about answering it until it was too late. It makes very little difference now. Such a letter wouldn't seem important, since neither of them wanted to give up their career. Your godfather didn't ask her to wait for him, I gather.'

'It was so long ago,' Janet said. 'We are not in a position to judge. Things were different in those days—there had been a war and people had to think a lot before they married. The man had to be sure that he had something substantial to offer before he took on such a commitment. I think that was the way it was.'

'No doubt,' he agreed, 'but it doesn't alter the present situation as I see it. I will not have you rushing off to Salzburg to confront my mother until I have seen her myself and explained everything.'

She drew back from the anger in his eyes.

'What will you tell her, Stephen?' she demanded. 'Will you say that Richard has forfeited any right to see her again? Will you tell her that love a second time around could never last, that it's all too late for them and you know it would never work? Will you try to convince her that she is better as she is now, the lonely Baroness living in a little *schloss* far from her native land and the man she first loved?'

'I'll do my best,' he said, 'but the final decision will be hers.'

'How adamant you are!' she cried. 'Does nothing matter to you except justice, as you call it?'

'Nothing,' he said, 'until I am absolutely sure that she will not be hurt again.'

'When will you see her?' she asked firmly. 'I can't stay here waiting for ever, but perhaps you don't want me to stay in your former home until you have time to examine your conscience,' she added with an anger to match his own.

'I am going to Salzburg this morning,' he said coldly.

'But you don't want me to come with you?'

'No,' he said. 'That would be a mistake. We must give her a choice—either to meet you in Salzburg later or to return here after you have gone. I think it's fair enough, don't you?'

'What do you expect me to say?' she asked. 'I can't fight you, Stephen—not over this, because I know how you must feel—but please, please think of Richard, too!'

He quickened his pace along the icy path.

'Your godfather is the least of my concerns,' he said, 'and I have still to solve the mystery of those threatening phone calls.'

'You won't trace them back to Richard,' she assured him. 'I know him too well!'

He opened the heavy door of the *schloss* to let her pass into the warmth of the hall.

'I know you have a high regard for him, but so, apparently, had my mother until he let her down so disgracefully,' he said.

'Stephen!' She put a detaining hand on his arm. 'Promise me you won't stand in their way if your mother wants to see him.'

He looked beyond her into the raftered hall.

'How could I do that?' he asked dispassionately. 'It will be her own decision in the end.'

'Then I can only hope it will be in Richard's favour,' she declared.

They were alone in the hall for a moment.

'What will you do with yourself while I'm away?' he asked.

'Pack,' she said. 'I couldn't stay here a moment longer if you come back from Salzburg with a negative answer.'

The silence between them was suddenly electric, and then Sophia came towards them from the foot of the stairs.

'That will be up to you, Janet,' he said before his cousin reached them. 'I have no desire to keep you here against your will.'

'What was all that about?' Sophia asked as he walked away.

'It was—nothing.' Janet didn't want to discuss their argument with anyone, least of all Sophia.

'Why does Stephen want to keep you here if you would rather leave?' Sophia persisted. 'Does he want you to marry him?'

Janet's laugh was a small, hurt cry.

'That must have been furthest from his thoughts,' she declared. 'There is no reason why he should want me at all.'

'If you say so!' Sophia shrugged. 'But it did look as if you had been arguing,' she added, unwilling to let the matter drop. 'A lovers' tiff, I imagined.'

Janet moved towards the half-opened door of the dining-room.

'It was nothing like that, Sophia,' she said. 'Stephen and I were never lovers.'

'Did you meet for the first time on the Orient Express?'

Janet drew a deep breath.

'Almost for the first time.'

'What do you mean "almost"?'

'We had met once before in my godfather's office in London.'

Sophia's eyes sharpened.

'That was a coincidence,' she suggested. 'Meeting again on the train.'

'It was how it was,' Janet assured her, crossing to the sideboard to collect the first course of her belated breakfast.

'You were out early,' Sophia observed. 'Did you hope to meet Stephen at the stables?'

'No. I wondered if Wolfgang could take me to Uttendorf or somewhere where I could get the Salzburg bus.'

'Behind Stephen's back?'

A bright flush rose into Janet's cheeks.

'If you like,' she said. 'I didn't want him to feel obliged to take me if he wanted to do something else.'

'I thought he might want a day's serious skiing,' said Sophia, helping herself to apple juice, 'but apparently not. He is going back to Salzburg to see his mother.'

'Yes, I know.'

Sophia's eyebrows shot up.

'You know?' she repeated. 'Then why didn't you ask him to take you?'

Janet sat down at the table with the bowl of cornflakes she had collected from the sideboard.

'Because he wanted to go alone.'

Sophia sighed heavily.

'There's no knowing about men,' she declared. 'One day they can be all for you, the next they exclude you completely. Be warned about Stephen,' she added darkly. 'He will not be deflected from a decision once he has made it, and if it concerns his mother you may be sure you will come off second best. He feels he has to defend her against the world now that she is sick and more or less alone, and I dare say he would take her back to Paris with him if only she would go.'

Janet stared out of the window.

'It seems to me that the Baroness thinks of this as her home,' she said. 'Apparently she had been here a long time, and it has many memories for her.'

'It has memories for Stephen, too.' Sophia crunched through a spoonful of cornflakes. 'He came here each holiday from school in England when his mother was only my uncle's secretary.'

Janet looked down at her half-empty bowl, feeling that she had no appetite for the cereal, after all.

'You've known each other for a long time,' she said.

'For years and years,' Sophia agreed. 'We quarrelled a lot when we were younger, of course, but that was only natural because Stephen always thought of himself as Big Brother, telling me what to do. It may have been his sense of responsibility because he was so much older. I don't know. All I'm sure about is that I don't want to be taken care of, if you know what I mean. It's old-fashioned and I'm my own person. I want to make decisions for myself. That's why Mother and I don't agree very often.' She glanced over her shoulder, as if she expected Anastasia to be listening at the door. 'She would like me to marry Stephen, you know, because it would give her much more authority here if ever the Baroness decided to go.'

Janet rose to her feet, leaving the remainder of her breakfast untouched.

'No coffee?' Sophia asked, moving to the sideboard.

'I—well, just one cup.'

'Sit down again and we'll think of something to do,' Sophia invited.

'I think I ought to collect a few things together,' Janet said. 'I could be leaving tomorrow.'

'Without Stephen?'

Janet bit her lip.

'Without Stephen,' she agreed.

'How about a run in the snow?' Sophia suggested agreeably. 'You said you were keen to ski.'

'I could hardly learn in one day.'

'Of course not, but you could make a start. Once you've got the knack you never really forget. I'm not suggesting we should go on the high trails, but there are quite a few easy runs farther up the valley you could manage quite well.' She paused to consider. 'Don't say no, because I can't bear to be working in the kitchen when it's still perfect skiing weather outside,' she added.

'Your mother may need your help.'

'She's got Wolf,' Sophia declared. 'They're as thick as two thieves. Wolf dances to any tune she likes to play, while she treats him shamefully. One day, I tell her, the worm will turn, but she refuses to listen. She doesn't take much notice of what I say, anyway,' Sophia sighed. 'You see, I'm a girl and not important. Mama would have given all she possessed to have a son, but now she has only Wolf!'

'How far are we likely to go?' Janet asked. 'I'm not too well equipped.'

'Don't worry! We're almost the same size, so skis won't be a problem and you can borrow my red suit,' Sophia offered, to make sure of a companion on the piste. 'I'll wear the new one I bought yesterday in Salzburg. It's absolutely super! I wanted Stephen to see it, and he might even he back here before we return.'

Almost reluctantly Janet followed her up the staircase to her bedroom on the second floor. It was small and cramped because most of the first-floor rooms had been given over to their guests, a fact Sophia appeared to acccept without question.

'Not much space,' she said, 'but I'm hardly ever in it except to sleep. I'll find you some thermal socks,' she offered, rummaging in a drawer. 'Red or blue? You can have a choice.'

'Blue, please,' Janet said.

The room was in chaos, with skis stacked in a corner and assorted equipment on every available chair. Sophia sat down on the floor.

'As long as your feet are warm,' she advised, 'you'll be all right. Can you pass me some red socks. Thank you! I get them as presents all the time because everybody knows how keen I am. You'll find the red suit in that cupboard over there. It's trousers and an anorak, hopelessly old-fashioned now, but it will do you for a start.'

She was struggling into her own one-piece, a lovely creation worthy of the most fashionable piste, with a deep white V in front reaching down to waist level and pale grey over all.

'You look absolutely stunning!' Janet assured her.

'D'you think Stephen will like it?' Sophia asked. 'It's really quite practical.'

'He's sure to,' Janet answered, thinking of Stephen on his way to Salzburg at that very moment to involve them all in his mother's decision.

Dressed in the red ski-suit, she glanced at her reflection in the ancient mirror beside the window.

'You look all right,' Sophia assured her, less generous in her praise. 'Anyway, it doesn't matter since we're not actually on show.'

When they reached the foot of the stairs, Anastasia was there to meet them.

'Where are you going?' she demanded. 'There are still guests in the house.'

'Only one,' her daughter reminded her. 'I'll be back in time to help with the dinner.'

'How thoughtful of you.' Anastasia made no reference to the new ski-suit. 'When did Stephen leave for Salzburg?'

'Early.' Sophia shouldered her skis. 'He seemed determined to go on his own this time,' she added thoughtfully. 'Maybe he had someone special to meet.'

'That would not surprise me,' said Anastasia tartly. 'He rarely takes anyone into his confidence and certainly not me!' She surveyed Janet in the red suit with evident disapproval. 'You are suddenly about to ski,' she observed.

'Oh, not very well,' Janet said. 'I'm an absolute beginner, but Sophia has offered to give me a lesson and I'm very grateful.'

'See that you do not go too far,' Anastasia cautioned, 'and watch out for avalanches. At this time of the year, when the snow is beginning to melt in the high mountains, they come down very easily and when they are least expected, and there are many accidents. We do not want—complications while you remain here,' she added stiffly.

'We won't take risks,' her daughter assured her, 'and we won't go far. You can send Wolf out to search for us if we don't return by four o'clock.'

'Have you something with you to eat?' Anastasia enquired.

'An apple and some bread. That will be enough,' Sophia decided in her eagerness to depart. 'We'll manage all right.' She paused at the door. 'You'll cope quite well,' she added.

'With Wolfgang's help,' her mother returned sourly.

'Faithful Wolf!' Sophia exclaimed as they went out into the sunshine. 'I wonder how long we can keep it that way. One day he may go off on his own and leave us flat.'

'Is that likely?'

'I'm not sure. Lately I think he's been restless, but mother has him by the fetlock. He loves horses and he enjoys the life here quite apart from the fact that he owes us so much. He's something of mystery, really,' Sophia mused as she bent to adjust Janet's skis. 'Mama came across him in Munich and decided to educate him because she had been left without a son of her own. I always thought it was strange, Mama taking a fancy to anyone, but she did. There you are!' She slid her feet into her own skis. 'We'll go slowly done the slope and keep to the valley road because you are so inexperienced. Follow me!'

Janet was nervous, but by the time they had gone carefully along the riverbank she found herself responding to the exhilaration of skimming over the snow like a bird. There were no real hazards on the flat, even surface of the road, and even when they began to climb she followed Sophia's instructions so carefully that she only came down twice, laughing as she got up covered in snow.

'You're getting the feel of it,' Sophia encouraged her. 'You make quite a good pupil.'

'Mostly on the flat!' Janet laughed. 'All the same, I feel I'm going to be addicted in the end. It's such a glorious experience swishing over the snow like this with nothing mechanical to propel you and the keen air on your face.'

'You're already a slave!' Sophia shook her hair free from its restricting band. 'We'll go higher and perhaps make the plateau where you'll have more scope.'

'How far is it?' Janet asked.

'Oh, not too far, and the higher we go the better the snow will be. It's beginning to be wet down here in the valley.'

'If you're sure I can manage,' Janet said.

'Of course you can. You're coming on better than I had expected. Relax a bit when you go downhill,' she advised. 'If you stiffen up, you'll risk a fall.'

Janet drew in a deep breath of sharp, cold air. It was wonderful out here with the sun already warm on their backs and what little wind there was caressing their cheeks. No wonder Stephen loved coming to the *schloss* from time to time; no wonder he was glad to think of his mother safely installed there!

When she looked about her she could imagine how lovely the valley would be in summer with all those rolling hills sweeping down to the river and the meadows starred with flowers. Little wooden huts dotted the hillside, their eaves heavy with snow which would soon melt to allow the cattle from the village to graze on the lush green grass beneath.

'We'll stop here,' Sophia decided, pulling up in front of one of them. 'It's time you had a rest.'

She swept snow from a bench in front of the hut and they sat down facing the sun.

'We've come a long way,' Janet reflected. 'I suppose I've managed quite well for a beginner.'

'Very well,' Sophia agreed, looking at her sideways. 'Of course, you had a lesson from Stephen.'

Janet could still remember the strength of Stephen's arms as he had lifted her, laughing, from the river trail which lay far beneath them now.

'I made a lot of mistakes,' she acknowledged, 'but it was fun.'

'Stephen is an excellent teacher. Impatient at times,' Sophia mused, 'if you take risks, but more or less tolerant. We've skied together for years, ever since Mama brought me back to the *schloss* to live. In some ways he was more like my brother than a cousin by marriage, and then, suddenly, all that changed.' She looked down across the pristine snow-fields. 'We became very fond of each other,' she added deliberately.

Janet's heart seemed to miss a beat.

'Not brother-and-sister fond,' Sophia went on. 'More—aware of each other as individuals, if you know what I mean.'

'Yes,' Janet said. 'I think I know.'

'At holiday times we were never off the piste, and there are runs across the mountains which take days to complete, so that's probably how we got to know each other so well.' Sophia's smile was reminiscent. 'Mama would never have allowed me to go with anyone else but Stephen. There was Wolf, of course, but she needed him at the *schloss*. I think she encouraged Stephen and me to be together, and I suppose she thought if we married eventually we could all live here together on more equal terms as a family.'

Janet turned to look at her at last.

'What went wrong?' she asked.

'Oh—Stephen didn't come so often. He was too busy building up his business connections in Paris.' Sophia unzipped the new ski-suit because it was now much warmer on the sun-drenched slopes. 'He kept in touch, of course, and I always knew he would return and everything would be like it was before. He is attractive, don't you think, in a rugged, he-man sort of way? And he certainly knows how I feel about him,' she rushed on, 'because I don't pretend about it. I think that's foolish, playing a sort of cat-and-mouse game with someone you adore.'

Janet stood up to look across the valley, feeling suddenly cold in spite of the warm sunshine on her face. Sophia was being quite open about her feelings, which was entirely in keeping with her ebullient character, seeing no reason why she should not declare her affection for her cousin without reserve, but what of Stephen? Why had he suddenly decided to stay away from Austria for so long, especially while his mother was still in residence at the *schloss*?

'Of course,' Sophia mused, 'he's much older than I am, but I don't think that really matters when you have a lot in common. Do you want to eat?' she asked in the same breath. 'I've got plenty in my haversack to keep us going till we get back for dinner.'

Janet watched as Sophia unpacked the small haversack she had carried on her back all the way up the gentle slope. It contained two of the nutty-tasting long loaves which were a speciality of the Schloss Erlach, a succulent-looking red sausage, four apples and a hunk of pink cheese cut into two.

'You've catered for a battalion!' Janet laughed, trying not to think about Stephen sharing the same sort of repast with his cousin on so many other occasions when the sun sparkled on the snow like crystal and the whole world around was theirs alone.

'Makes one feel hungry, all this fresh air and exercise,' Sophia declared, spreading butter on one of the loaves after she had passed the other one to Janet. 'The sausage is home-made.'

They ate slowly, munching a juicy apple afterwards as they considered their return to the *schloss*.

'You've done amazingly well,' Sophia reflected. 'Maybe we could tackle the high trail above the valley and go back by another way. Do you think you could?'

They had rested for the best part of an hour, but Janet could have lingered much longer in that sunny spot where everything seemed so peaceful and remote. She had thought a lot about Stephen while they sat there, and about his mother who had undoubtedly found peace at the *schloss*.

'Sophia,' she asked, 'what is the Baroness really like?'

'Oh—very beautiful and very elegant. Tall, like Stephen, and very slim,' Sophia said. 'She sang under the name of Alicia Von Erlach in Salzburg and her voice was lovely.'

A suspicion which had been taking shape in Janet's mind crystallised.

'If you had met her you would always remember her,' Sophia concluded, placing the remains of their al-fresco meal into the haversack.

'I think I already have. At least,' Janet amended, 'I think I have seen her with Stephen.'

Sophia looked surprised.

'Where?' she asked.

'In Salzburg—outside the Goldener Hirsch.' Janet was able to speak freely about the mistake she had made. 'I took her for an intimate friend.'

'But that was absurd!' Sophia protested. 'She's much, much older than Stephen—naturally.'

'I must have seen them in an indifferent light,' Janet decided. 'They were kissing each other goodbye. My mistake!' she acknowledged. 'What you have just said is perfectly true, Sophia, as far as beauty and elegance goes. I wondered who she was.'

'You were thinking she was Stephen's lover!' Sophia laughed. 'They are too alike to be anything but mother and son.'

Which was a comforting conclusion for Sophia, Janet thought, but a disturbing one as far as she was concerned, because she had long pictured Alice Silton as the sweet young girl Richard had first described to her. It would be far more difficult now to approach a mature woman who had made something of a success of her life and who might easily have already made up her mind about the future.

'We ought to go,' she said, brushing the breadcrumbs from her anorak. 'It's getting late. And, Sophia,' she added. 'I think we should go back the way we came.'

'Just as you like,' Sophia agreed, 'although we would be longer in the sun if we went by the high trail.'

Janet hesitated. Rested now, she felt quite capable of a longer run, provided there were no hazards along the way.

'You know how inexperienced I am,' she warned, 'but—'

'It's not really so much fun going back the same way,' Sophia told her. 'I wouldn't take you if I didn't feel you could manage it.'

'I'm flattered!' Janet was ready to go. 'Will you lead the way?'

On the edge of the high snowfields the going was good and easy. Criss-cross trails suggested other skiers in their immediate vicinity, although they were nowhere to be seen, and once more the exhilaration of the snows blotted out any sense of danger for Janet, at least as they sped along on a smoothly descending slope until eventually they reached the treeline, where a stand of firs loomed up darkly ahead of them.

'Do you need another rest?' Sophia asked. 'I've two more apples in my rucksack.'

They munched the apples while they looked down into the valley below.

'Is there another village down there?' Janet asked. 'I thought I saw smoke.'

'Yes. The *schloss* is sort of between them, but we don't have to go right down to Arnberg,' Sophia explained. 'We can cut across the top fields and go down that way. You're not too tired?'

'I'll probably ache in every limb tomorrow,' predicted Janet, 'but it will have been well worth while. Do we go now?'

Sophia tossed the core of her apple as far as she could down the slope.

'Follow me!' she directed. 'Keep as close as you can till we are clear of the wood, and it's easy enough from there. When I pull up you pull up, remember. There's a bit of a dip on the far side of the wood—nothing to worry about, you understand—but I'll give you a demonstration when we get to it.'

She shot off, weaving expertly down the slope while Janet followed her with all her confidence restored. She had been on her feet for a good part of the day and, so far, nothing had gone wrong. She had found the sport far more invigorating than she had expected, surprised by her own enthusiasm and the patience of her instructor. Sophia was indeed an expert!

Skirting the wood, they came to the hollow ground where Sophia drew up.

'Watch me!' she commanded, dipping rapidly into the first hollow and out again on the far side before she made a quick turn to come back. 'You have to have enough speed to take you up again on the other side and over the top. Do you understand what I mean?'

'Yes.' Janet bit her lip. 'I suppose it's quite easy.'

'Once you get going,' Sophia agreed. 'Don't hesitate, and remember to go down fast.'

'I'll do my best,' Janet promised. 'Are you going first?'

'If you like,' Sophia agreed. 'Remember what I told you and keep your head down. It couldn't be easier!'

With a swish of skis she had gone, down into the hollow and up and over the top on the other side.

'There's no need for you to make a mountain out of a molehill,' Janet muttered to herself as she followed close behind. 'It's all experience.'

Down she went in a clean swish of snow and up on the far side almost to the top. She wasn't going to make it and suddenly she was nervous. I must! I must! she thought in desperation. I can't fall back now!

But she was falling, sliding back down the crisp snowbank to the bottom of the hollow where she was suddenly tossed aside like a rag doll, her skis stuck in the snow, her arm bent back under her while an excruciating pain shot through her shoulder.

For a moment she could neither see nor reason. Soft snow was falling in a little flurry from the bank down which she had returned so inelegantly, and the world about her was darker than she remembered.

Drawing a deep breath, she tried to get up, remembering all the instructions she had been given, only to fall back with a sharp cry of pain when she tried to find her sticks now buried in the snow. When the pain subsided she saw that her right arm was hanging loosely by her side.

Panic seized her because she could do nothing to help herself.

'Sophia,' she cried, 'help me!'

It seemed an age before her companion's head appeared above the rim of the hollow.

'You must try to get up,' Sophia said. 'There are always those little hurts when you first learn. Do you want me to come down?'

'Please,' Janet gasped. 'I—seem to have lost my arm——

Sophia was already by her side.

'Nonsense!' she said. 'You've probably just wrenched it a bit. Oh——'

'What is it?' To Janet, the pain seemed to be worse than before. 'What's happened, Sophia? Is it broken?'

'I—don't think so.' Sophia looked at her and then up at the slope of the hollow. 'I can't do anything about it on my own,' she decided. 'I'll have to go for help.'

CHAPTER SIX

THE hollow grew cold as the sun went down and the snow changed from white to grey. Janet lay quite still, remembering what Sophia had said, while all she could see over the rim of her prison were the green tips of the stand of pines speckled with white, and the azure sky above her turning slowly darker as she waited.

There was no real pain, only a dullness in her body which seemed to be centred in her injured arm. To move it proved impossible.

How long she lay there she did not know. A great silence seemed to envelop the whole world, closing her in as time passed and no one came to her rescue. She could feel the snow penetrating the gap between her trousers and the red anorak, conscious of the fact that she had slid to the very bottom of the hollow without really feeling anything. Which meant that her sticks were more than a yard away from her and therefore useless. She could not see them because they were behind her, and even if she had attempted to reach them she would never have been able to make the run to the top.

The silence numbed her, making time of little consequence. It passed and she was still there.

When she heard the voices, it seemed that she had been waiting for an eternity. It was clearly Sophia's voice which reached her first, carrying over the snow.

'She's down there, in the hollow beside the trees.'

Relief and thankfulness poured in on Janet like a reviving tide as she heard a man's sterner tones answering his companion. Wolfgang, she thought, closing her eyes.

When she opened them again there was a swish of metal on snow as a dark figure swept round her, coming to an abrupt halt where she lay. It was Stephen.

His bulk seemed to fill up all the hollow as he bent over her.

'I've got to get you on to your feet,' he said, reaching for her sticks. 'We have to see what the damage is.'

Lifting her gently, he steadied her against himself.

'Oh, Stephen!' she gasped, but that was all.

He held her for a moment of breathless ecstasy, her head against his shoulder while he assessed the damage to her arm, and when he put her away from him she saw his face clearly for the first time. Full of concern, it looked almost grey in the rapidly fading light.

He told her, then, what he had to do.

'We've got to get your arm back into place,' he explained. 'It will hurt like hell, but you have to trust me.'

Before she had time to answer, he jerked her shoulder back into its socket. It was the swift action of the expert performing a task he had done many times before, but the sudden, excruciating pain took her breath away.

'That was cruel!' she accused him, the tears filling her eyes.

'There was no other way,' he said grimly as he held her for a moment longer. 'You would have resisted me if I had been gentle with you. As it is,' he added with one arm still around her, 'you are going to have a pretty sore arm for a day or two, but it will mend. Meanwhile, keep off the slopes,' he warned with a spark of anger in his eyes. 'This is no time to learn to ski, and Sophia knows that. When the snow begins to melt there's also a danger of avalanches, so be advised.'

He was more angry than she would have expected; angry with Sophia who should never have suggested such a foolish adventure in the first place, and angry with her for allowing herself to be led astray. Or was it perhaps because a more serious accident could have kept her longer at the *schloss* than he had intended?

She did her best to hide the tears that had gathered in her eyes.

'You're going to be all right,' he promised. 'It's been a shock, but there's nothing broken, thank heavens! Can you stand up straight—stretch your back? Good,' he decided, 'you're all in one piece, and now you can help me to get you out of here.'

He was being practical because he had seen her distress, and she swept away the tears with the back of her hand.

'Tell me what to do,' she said.

Sophia skimmed towards them down the slope.

'It wasn't very pleasant, was it?' she said, looking at the restored arm. 'It has to be done like that—quickly and without fuss—otherwise it might not be so effective. Do you feel all right otherwise?'

Janet nodded.

'I'm just a bit stiff—and cold,' she admitted, still clinging to Stephen's guiding hand.

'What we have to do is get you to the top in easy stages,' he explained. 'Hold on to me, and Sophia will put her skis behind you as we climb. You won't be able to use your right arm so you'll have to put most of your weight on your stick on the other side. Don't worry about it; just take it slowly, one step at a time, and we'll get there.'

His arm round her for extra support, they made the laborious ascent.

'It's like climbing the Matterhorn when you first look up,' Sophia joked, 'but we'll get you to the top, never fear! Just hang on to Stephen and remember I'm right behind you.'

'That will be a doubtful comfort to her,' Stephen remarked drily. 'You should have known better than this.'

'Yes, I'm sorry!' Sophia sounded contrite. 'But we were both so keen to go.'

'Yes, please don't think it was entirely Sophia's fault,' Janet managed. 'I was equally to blame for wanting to learn, in the first place, since there is really no future in it for me.'

'That's defeatist,' he said, 'but maybe you should stick to the nursery slopes next time till you gain experience.'

They were almost at the top, and then suddenly they were over the rim with the sun still there on the higher slopes, veiled now as it dipped towards the horizon. Then something Janet had never seen before coloured the snow around them a vivid pink, sending shafts of light to every corner of the valley as the sun disappeared behind the ridge of the western mountains beyond the trees.

'I've never seen anything so beautiful!' she exclaimed as Stephen put a guiding hand under her elbow. 'I'll always remember this.'

Their progress on the regular ski-trail was necessarily slow, but as they neared the *schloss* Sophia swept ahead.

'Better prepare Mama for an invalid!' she called back.

'Please don't!' Janet begged, but Sophia had already gone.

'I wish she hadn't done that,' Janet added to her silent companion as they followed the well-marked trail to the *schloss*. 'I don't intend to be a nuisance, Stephen. If I had broken a leg or anything like that it would be different, but I can manage without the use of one hand.'

'You'd better decide about that tomorrow,' he advised. 'I don't mean that you should take things easy, but you're not in a fit state to travel very far.'

She had to know about the Baroness, whether he had met her in Salzburg or not, and what they had decided.

'Did you see your mother?' she asked. 'You must have come back fairly early.'

'We had lunch together at the Carlton.' He helped her up the incline to the *schloss*, well aware of what she was waiting for him to tell her. 'You must understand that she was deeply shocked, although she already knew that Richard Cosgrave was trying to find her.'

'I—would she agree to see me?' Janet asked the question with very little hope of receiving the reply she desired.

'I didn't ask her that. She must have time to make up her own mind, to consider what she really wants to do.'

'Yes,' she said, 'I know that, but I thought——' She paused, facing him with an unspoken question on her eyes.

'You thought it would be easy,' he returned, 'but no one will persuade her against her will, Jan. I know her well enough to be convinced of that, at least. Twenty-eight years is a long time, and she agrees that she has changed. She had to battle against a great many odds, and she thinks it may have hardened her.'

'What do *you* think?' she asked. 'You probably know her better than anyone.'

He looked towards the *schloss*.

'I've seen her make decisions in the past, some of them momentous, but it has never taken her long to reach a decision after she has weighed up the consequences. She has a very alert mind and a deep insight into human nature.'

'Are you saying she might consider seeing Richard in the end? Stephen, it is important to me,' she added urgently. 'I want to see him happy.'

'And I want to see my mother's peace of mind restored to her,' he returned. 'Anything that might prejudice that is a non-starter.'

'You're still thinking of those phone calls?'

'What else?'

'You know Richard had nothing to do with them!' she cried. 'How could he stoop so low when he loved her?'

He propelled he towards the heavily studded door of his former home.

'You're asking too many questions,' he said, 'but I can tell you that they have stopped since your godfather went to New York.'

'Which means you're still not convinced!' she cried. 'Stephen, I have given you my word. Richard wouldn't do anything like that.'

'I would hardly expect him to threaten her, hoping that she would return to England, if he really means what you say.'

'Which you doubt?' Tears dimmed her eyes because she was tired and in pain and bitterly disappointed that he refused to trust her. 'You've never been able to believe me or why I came here,' she accused him. 'You think I have some sort of axe to grind, but that isn't true. It was a straightforward job, something Richard would have done for himself if he hadn't been obliged to go to New York, but I don't expect you to believe that, either. You're completely prejudiced, completely insenstive to anyone's feelings but your own!'

He led her into the hall.

'You're tired,' he said almost gently. 'I'll speak to my mother again in the morning.'

'If she will see me I'll go to Salzburg,' Janet offered. 'I can't stay here, Stephen, knowing how much you distrust me,' she added, straightening to her full height as he unstrapped her skis. 'I'll leave as soon as possible and go back to the Goldener Hirsch. It will only be for a couple of nights, and I ought to report back to London.'

'There's nothing to stop you from phoning from here,' he suggested. 'We have a full telex arrangement with the village post office, but perhaps you would rather do it from Salzburg?'

He had accepted her departure from the *schloss*, glad,

perhaps, that this painful episode in the saga of his life had ended, and she turned her back on him to prevent him seeing the full extent of her hurt. She had said she would go and she would be forced to keep her word, but to go now would be to lose him as Richard had lost his one and only love all those years ago in London.

In her room at last, she stood for a moment looking out at a world that had gone suddenly dark.

'Richard,' she whispered uncertainly into the night, 'I know now just how you felt!'

The watching stars pricking out in the darker blue had little comfort to offer her. Far away and remotely cold above the snowfields, they looked down at her without pity, knowing that she was in love with Stephen.

By the following morning her shoulder had stiffened considerably, slowing her progress as she tried to dress. Zip fasteners were impossible, especially at the back, so she finally settled for a front-buttoning top over the skirt she had worn in Salzburg to walk to the Getreidegasse in search of the Dietrichs' shop. It all seemed a very long time ago, yet only days had passed, days in which Stephen had coloured all her thoughts. He would shadow her future for a long, long time, she realised, until she had learned to forget him, and that might take as long as it had taken Richard, who had never really forgotten. Was she treading the same path, in spite of her determination not to care?

'Can I come in?' Sophia asked, tapping on her door. 'I wondered if you might need some help.'

'I feel a fraud,' Janet assured her. 'I'm not as badly injured as I thought. It's all just an inconvenience not being able to tie up a shoelace or pull on a zip if it's at the back.'

'I once had to wear a surgical collar for a week or two for a neck injury,' Sophia told her as she helped her with the buttons on the top. 'It was awful! Everything that went over my head was a disaster, and I had to eat standing up!'

Janet laughed.

'Stephen admitted that it would be uncomfortable for a day or two,' she remarked.

'He's gone back to Salzburg.' Sophia glanced in the mirror. 'He may have gone to see the Baroness again.'

'I think he has.' Janet forced a smile. 'In fact, I'm almost sure.'

'Is she still at the Carlton?' Sophia wanted to know.

'I think so. I first saw them saying goodbye outside the Goldener Hirsch,' Janet mused.

Sophia nodded.

'Ah, yes! She often goes there. It is a meeting-place for artists when they are performing at the special music weeks, and she has many friends.'

Yet, in some ways, Janet imagined that the Baroness Von Erlach might be lonely.

'I'd like to meet her,' she said. 'I think Stephen might be able to arrange it.' When there was no immediate reply, she added slowly, 'I have to leave here, Sophia. I have to go back to London.'

'Oh?' Sophia turned from the mirror. 'Perhaps we can meet in London, in that case. You know we are going there quite soon. It's something of a ritual with Mama, goodness knows why, except that she's always done it ever since I can remember. London or Paris—one or the other. It's as if a town cancels out the boredom of life in a remote *schloss* where she has to work like a peasant to earn a living.'

'She'll come back refreshed in spirit, at least,' Janet suggested. 'Personally, I'd never want to spend my time in a city if I could live here.'

'Not even in Paris? Sophia suggested with a quick glance at her. 'I thought you and Stephen were becoming quite fond.'

She paused at the open door, waiting for Janet to deny or confirm her supposition.

'That would be—impossible,' Janet said with an attempt at firmness. 'We hardly know one another.'

Sophia tossed back her hair with a quick movement of her head.

'I think, if you had stayed longer, it could have happened,' she predicted. 'But then, we'll never know, will we? Does Stephen know you're leaving?' she asked.

'I think he expects me to go.'

'Shall I break the news to Mama? You're our only remaining guest,' Sophia pointed out.

'I'll tell her when I come down,' Janet decided. 'I know I'm late, but perhaps she will excuse me when she sees how handicapped I am.'

'Don't expect any pity,' Sophia warned. 'Mama considers all skiers to be mad, and she'll probably think you deserve what you got, although she may even tell you she's sorry.'

Clinging to the wrought-iron banister rail, Janet went slowly down the stairs to the hall. The quietness of the *schloss* emphasised Stephen's absence, and even Sophia had vanished. I like her and I don't, Janet thought, although I'm sure there is no real harm in her.

Anastasia emerged from the shadows.

'I hear you wish to leave,' she said. 'When will you go?'

'Tomorrow, I think.' Janet drew in a quick breath. 'I must return to Salzburg. Will you let me have my bill, please?'

'With pleasure.' Anastasia stood her ground. 'How long will you stay in Salzburg?' she asked.

'A day—perhaps two. I have no further reason for being there after that,' Janet admitted.

'You came for Mozart, perhaps?'

'No. Though I am fond of music.'

'I have no ear for it, nor the time to study it,' Anastasia returned. 'Some people make it their life.'

'It can be such a full life,' Janet said, 'and a rewarding

career.'

'You have to be at the peak for that—right at the top of the tree.' Anastasia busied herself with her morning duties, rearranging a curtain here and there, inspecting the hearth to make sure that Wolfgang had cleared out the wood ash from the night before and polished the wrought-iron fire-basket when he had re-set the logs. 'My sister-in-law has become quite well known in Salzburg since she decided to take my brother's name,' she added drily. 'No doubt it has helped her to succeed, but perhaps it is a little late for fame. Her voice is not strong enough for opera, but she does well enough on the concert platform.'

Eager to find out all she could about Alice Silton, Janet lingered in the sun-filled hall.

'I understand that she has been ill,' she said.

Anastasia flicked an imaginary speck of dust from the high mantelpiece.

'She never had the stamina of the Von Erlachs,' she announced. 'Always it was a cold she was having or an infection of the throat, and then she could not sing at all. She had been too long in Paris to cope with our mountain air, but my brother would not be told. Towards the end of his life she had a great influence on him.' Again the duster flicked across the heavy mantelpiece. 'Old men can be easily led.'

'Perhaps your brother found her a great comfort and a true companion,' Janet suggested. 'Perhaps they both needed a shoulder to lean on.'

Anastasia tucked the duster into the capacious pocket of her overall.

'He could have depended on his family if he had wished it,' she declared frigidly. 'He could have depended on me. I was a Von Erlach—of the same blood.'

It would be difficult to understand anything Anastasia did, Janet thought as she pushed open the dining-room door, but it was not and never could be her affair. Anastasia, like

Sophia and Stephen, were all part of an amazing interlude in her life which she could not have imagined two weeks ago, and no doubt they would pass as quickly out of it. She had asked for her bill and as soon as it was settled in the morning she would leave.

'Wolfgang will drive you to the village when you are ready in the morning,' Anastasia said, following her into the room. 'There is a bus service from there to Salzburg twice at week.'

So, that was settled. No waiting for Stephen's return, hoping that he might offer to take her as far as the Goldener Hirsch!

'Do you think I could make a phone call?' she asked. 'I will have to book into a hotel in Salzburg and the Goldener Hirsch is the only one I know.'

'You are sure to be comfortable there,' said Anastasia drily. 'It is one of Salzburg's top grade hotels. Very expensive, of course.'

'I won't be staying for more than a night or two.' Janet stood before the sideboard looking down at the array of covered dishes set aside for her selection without any real appetite. 'Perhaps not even as long as that,' she added, her throat suddenly constricted as she sat down on a chair with her back to the window.

'Is there nothing to satisfy you?' Anastasia asked, affronted. 'You do not like what we provide?'

'Please don't think that,' Janet begged. 'It's just that—I seem to be a little shaken after my accident yesterday and I'm not very hungry. I'll have some apple juice and some of your delightful warm bread, if I may?'

'You will please yourself,' Anastasia told her. 'Everybody else has eaten.' She felt the copper percolator. 'It is hot,' she decided, 'but if you wish for more Wolfgang will bring it from the kitchen. The telephone is in the hall,' she added on her way to the door.

A glass of apple juice and two cups of coffee later, Janet felt refreshed, but what was she to do with her day? Her last day at the *schloss*! Sophia was nowhere to be seen when she went out into the walled garden in search of her, and she turned back into the hall to make her phone call to Salzburg.

When she had found the number she stood in the small curtained alcove where she had found the instrument, reluctant to use it even now that she had finally made up her mind. The silence everywhere seemed to press down upon her, deepening her pain because she knew that once she had lifted the receiver and dialled the number there would be no turning back. She would have taken an inevitable step towards the future. She thought of the journey to London ahead of her as a long pilgrimage in search of something she would never find, although at the end of it she would be able to give Richard the hope he wanted. She could tell him where he could find Alice, where to write to her, and perhaps, eventually, where to come to meet her at last.

Determinedly she put through her call.

'Yes, that will be quite all right,' she was told. A room would be reserved for her the following day.

Finality, she thought. The first step away from the *schloss* and Stephen, who might even now be planning his own return to Paris.

When Sophia failed to appear by eleven o'clock, Janet put on her coat and fur-lined boots to go for a walk, the sun enticing her along the riverbank where already the trees were in full leaf. Dappled light and shade lay on the ice-cold water, with little drifts of snow sailing down like white puffs of cotton wool in the shallows. Spring was a magic time everywhere, she thought, a new beginning, a blossoming promise, a hope.

She looked up as an inquisitive mountain goat sprang down from the bank ahead of her to regard her with sombre eyes and his head on one side. Are you alone, he seemed to ask, and why should that be on a morning like this? When he shook his head the heavy bell on his collar jangled discordantly, and she watched him walk away with an odd feeling of regret. There seemed to be nobody in the whole valley but herself, until she saw Wolfgang coming towards her. He had been herding the goats who were now walking in the shallows, obviously impervious to the cold.

'Have you come a long way, Wolf?' she asked, remembering that she had not seen him at the *schloss*. 'You have a lot of work to do.'

'More than enough,' he said, smacking a truant goat with the stick he carried. 'I do almost everything at the *schloss*.'

'But you like the work?' she suggested, supposing that he must find some sort of satisfaction in his job. 'You are quite happy here?'

'I'm happy enough,' he said, 'but I could also wish that things were different.' A sullen look crept into his eyes. 'Always I have to do as I am told. There is no freedom.'

'Perhaps you would prefer to work in a city,' she suggested.

He considered the idea, his dark brows drawn.

'Not in a city,' he decided.

'Not in London—or Paris?'

He shook his head.

'They are too full of noise,' he said. 'What I want is to teach.'

'Children, do you mean?'

'Children, who are——' He paused. 'Handicapped is not the word I want,' he decided.

'Deprived?' Janet suggested.

He nodded, looking up at her with genuine interest in his eyes.

'Those that have no real home of their own,' he said.

'Does Frau Waldburger know how you feel?' Janet asked.

He shook his head.

'She does not understand. She gave me a good education,' he acknowledged, 'but she cannot give me love.'

'Wolf,' Janet said, genuinely touched, 'I'm sorry! I wish there were some way I could help you.'

'There is no way,' he said. 'I am always depending on her for everything.'

'What age are you, Wolf?' she asked.

'Nineteen.'

She turned to walk back with him by the way she had come.

'Have you spoken about this to the Baroness?' she asked.

The question electrified him. He stood on the path in the midst of the herd of goats, looking as if he would never speak again.

'Or Mr Stephen?' she suggested. 'He might be able to help you.'

'How could I speak to them?' His voice was no more than a strangled whisper. 'How could I ever speak to the Baroness or ask her a favour?'

'Surely she would not be unkind?'

He prodded the goats with his stick, herding the wayward ones back on to the path.

'I could not ask her,' he said, turning away, 'and if she was kind I would be ashamed.'

They walked a few paces in silence.

'Did you come to the *schloss* with Frau Waldburger?' Janet asked.

He nodded.

'I have been with her many years, almost as long as I can remember.'

'And before that?' she prompted.

'I was in a home for deprived children. I have no clear memory of it, but I can tell you I was happy.'

Janet gazed up at the *schloss*.

'You have many privileges here, Wolf,' she pointed out.

'So long as I obey and do what Frau Waldburger says.'

She thought that he was not servile by nature, and Anastasia would be a hard taskmistress, but at nineteen years of age he would be perfectly entitled to break away unless there were some other, stronger bond between them.

'Perhaps she thinks about you as the son she never had,' she suggested carefully. 'Could that be it?'

'She does not trust me like a son and I could not expect her to do so,' he answered. 'I am willing to go on obeying her up to a point.'

They had reached the incline up to the *schloss* where a car stood before the heavily studded door. Janet recognised the Mercedes, her heart pounding heavily in her breast.

'The young master has returned,' Wolf said, heading his unruly flock towards the side of the house. 'You will not speak of this conversation we have had to anyone?'

'It can do no harm,' she objected. 'If I asked Mr Stephen to help, I'm sure he would.'

Wolf looked round at her, his eyes flaming.

'I tell you not to ask,' he said almost threateningly. 'It will only mean trouble for me.'

Janet turned her head away. Poor Wolf, she thought, how can he ever be happy, feeling the way he does?

Before she opened the door she stood for a moment to regain her breath. Stephen had returned earlier than she had expected, and she didn't know how to meet him. Then resolutely she pushed open the door and walked into the hall.

Stephen was standing at the fire pulling off his gloves, and on the other side of the hearth a tall woman in a grey, fur-lined cloak was warming her hands at the glow. She was as tall as Stephen but very slim, and there could be no doubt about their relationship now that she was seeing the Baroness at close quarters at last. The same breadth of forehead, the same fearless grey-blue eyes challenged her across the hall, and after the barest hesitation Stephen's unforgettable smile lit up his mother's face. This was the elegant lady Janet had seen him with outside the Goldener Hirsch.

The Baroness came towards her, hands outstretched.

'I have no need for Stephen to make an introduction,' she said. 'You are Janet. He has told me all about you.' Cool, slender fingers gripped hers as Janet found herself looking at Alice Silton as she now was, thinking that the signs of frailty about her only served to enchance her mature beauty. Close to, there were lines on her face, lines of living and laughter and tears. 'If he had told me before you left Salzburg, we could have met there.'

'I was still searching for you then.' Janet wondered just how much Stephen had told her. 'I'm sorry if it has brought you back before you intend to come.'

'It is no distance,' the Baroness said, 'and this is my home. In a week—perhaps two—I would have returned anyway.' She took off the grey cloak, laying it aside on a nearby chair. 'We have just arrived,' she explained. 'Less than five minutes ago, and my luggage is still to bring in.'

Which meant that she had come to stay.

'You must want your home to yourself,' Janet said. 'I'll be leaving in the morning, but—but I'm so glad I've met you.'

Stephen spoke for the first time.

'There is no need for you to go to the Goldener Hirsch,' he said. 'You can stay here equally well till you go back to England.'

'I think it would be better if I went in the morning,' Janet decided.

The Baroness turned from the fire to look at her.

'You have hurt your arm, I hear,' she said. 'There is no reason why you should not stay here till it mends.'

'I haven't found it much of an inconvenience,' Janet said, not looking at Stephen because she was going to refuse his mother's hospitality, 'and I must return to London as quickly as possible.' Her eyes held the older woman's reflective look. 'Richard relies on me to be there when he is away for any length of time.'

'Ah, yes—Richard!' The Baroness removed her grey mink turban. 'He is well, I suppose, when he is busy in New York.' She glanced across the hearth at her son. 'Stephen, can you find Wolf to help you with my luggage? There's quite a lot of it.'

Stephen looked at Janet as if he were about to say something more, but at that moment Anastasia chose to appear. She stood in the archway leading to the kitchen, her face taut with frustration as she contemplated the new arrivals.

'Is there not a telephone in this house?' she asked. 'At least you could have phoned to say you were coming.'

'We did try to get in touch, Anastasia,' the Baroness returned patiently, 'and got no reply. Perhaps you were out somewhere, or there was some other distracting noise.'

'I would have heard the bell,' her sister-in-law returned, refuting her suggestion immediately. 'I am not yet deaf, Alicia. You ought to know that.'

'Then I am sorry. The bell must not ring loudly enough to alert you when you are in a distant part of the house.'

Anastasia froze her with a look.

'I have my duties to do,' she reminded her coldly. 'I cannot sit all day in the hall waiting for the telephone to ring.'

'We must have an extension, in that case—even two,' the Baroness suggested. 'Where are Wolf and Gretchen?'

'Wolfgang is bringing in the goats and Gretchen has the afternoon off to visit her grandmother.'

That said, Anastasia turned on her heel, marching back in the direction of the kitchens, while the Baroness gathered up her hat and gloves, making slowly towards the staircase.

'I will see you in half an hour,' she said, looking down at Janet from the first stair, 'and we will talk.'

Stephen and Wolf passed Janet on their way up with the Baroness's luggage. It looked regally expensive, with a well known logo on the space under each handle, all of it matching grey, as were her knee-high fur-lined boots. She was beautiful beyond comparison, Janet thought, but cold.

It was a first assessment which she was later to regret, but it seemed in that moment of their meeting that Alice Von

Erlach was decidedly wary about her.

Wondering what impression Stephen had conveyed to her, what personal reaction he had communicated, she went out again into the snow-covered grounds, walking for a while in the shelter of the walled garden to adjust her thoughts. It was peaceful there and she was alone until suddenly she became aware of someone watching her from the arched gateway. When she turned, the sun dazzling her for a moment, she saw that it was Stephen.

He came swiftly towards her.

'How does your arm feel?' he asked.

'You promised me it would stiffen up, and it has,' she said lightly. 'Otherwise, it isn't very painful. Thank you, Stephen,' she added, 'for all you did.'

He brushed her appreciation aside.

'Why have you suddenly decided to leave—behind my back?' he demanded. 'Was it too much to ask you to stay here till I got back?'

'You didn't ask.'

'No.' He hesitated as if he were about to tell her something of importance, and then he said deliberately, 'I had other things on my mind.'

'More important things?' She looked at him steadily. 'Yes, perhaps I can understand. Helping Richard to find your mother isn't important to you. It is to me.'

'My reason had nothing to do with Richard, nor with you,' he said, dark anger veiling his eyes. 'It has to do with my mother's welfare, her happiness, if you like. I made myself responsible for that long ago, and until I can be sure that she can at least live here peacefully, I'm determined not to think of anything else.'

'I'm sure you won't,' she agreed, turning her head away, 'and I think I know how you feel.'

He gripped her by the shoulders, compelling her to face him.

'You can't know anything about it,' he said roughly 'You came here knowing nothing of the truth, and now that your mission is completed you are quite ready to go back to London without thinking of all the damage you might have done in the process.'

'Damage?' She tried to release herself, hurt and anger forcing her words out before she could stifle them. 'How could I possibly have changed your life, or your mother's for that matter? I came for one reason and one reason only,' she rushed on. 'To help Richard, and I told you why right from the beginning. I *owed* him this, Stephen. I owed it to him for years and years of constant love and care, for a childhood that might have been unhappy and wasn't, and I couldn't let him down over such a little thing as this.'

'A little thing?' he repeated, staring down at her. 'Is that what you think of it?' He released her with a suddenness which made her step back as if in self-defence. 'Well, we won't argue about it,' he decided. 'After you have spoken to my mother you will be free to go back to London to report to Richard Cosgrave and make your future plans.'

'I have no plans—not in the way you mean,' she said quietly, 'but I am free, Stephen. Free to do what I want about Richard, for example. I mean to ask the Baroness to meet him somewhere to discuss the past.'

'I knew you intended to do that,' he allowed, 'and I can't stop you. She came back with me this afternoon fully prepared to talk, even to see your point of view, but I will not promise you anything. She is bound to be confused over all this—and over those damned elusive telephone calls which constantly urge her to return to England, where she belongs. They have played havoc with her nerves because they have persisted for so long, and my fear is that they may drive her away from the *schloss* for good.'

'I'm sorry, Stephen,' she said, laying a sympathetic hand on his arm. 'I wish I could help you in that respect, at least.'

Deliberately he shook her hand from his sleeve.

'I don't think I need your help,' he said. 'Nor anyone's. This is something I have to do for myself. When you are ready tomorrow morning, I shall take you back to Salzburg to the Goldener Hirsch.'

Were they quarrelling? Was he telling her as plainly as he could that she had outstayed her welcome at the *schloss*, just as Anastasia had done that morning, helping her in every way possible to bow out of their lives for good? Were they quarrelling blindly and foolishly, just as Alice and Richard had done all those years ago while they were still in love with each other?

In love? Yes, Richard had been in love then, as he was now, but Stephen had never been in love with her. Janet turned towards the arched gateway with all the bitterness of rejection gnawing at her heart.

'If I can't help you,' she said, 'if all this is so—private as far as you are concerned, I'm glad that I can go. It would only add to my disillusionment to outstay my welcome, but please remember that I didn't ask to come here. You brought me, Stephen, probably because you didn't trust me when you knew why I had come to Austria in the first place, and all I can offer in my defence is the fact that I never wanted to hurt the Baroness or cause you pain.'

Closing the wrought-iron gate firmly behind her, she left him standing there in the sunshine, his face tense with irresolution, his hands tightly clenched by his sides. He had refused to follow her, even to argue with her further, and that seemed to be the end of any meaningful contact between them.

Unhappily she made her way back to the *schloss*, feeling that success in Richard's cause no longer meant quite the same to her, yet she had to pursue it because it was why she had come to Austria in the beginning.

CHAPTER SEVEN

WAITING in the hall for the Baroness to come down to her, she stood by the fire that Wolfgang had lit earlier, watching the sparks shoot up from the crackling logs, like all her hopes disappearing up the chimney to fly away in the cold, bleak wind of an early spring day.

'Will you come with me into the library? There is also a fire lit in there and we shall be alone.'

The Baroness had come quietly down the staircase without her noticing, and was standing only a few paces away. Janet turned immediately.

'I didn't hear you come down,' she apologised. 'I was daydreaming.'

'We all do that from time to time,' Alice Von Erlach said, smiling a little. 'It's often our outlet for disillusionment and frustration, and personally I think we might be lost without such an escape, although it could never be called realistic. It's an indulgence we allow ourselves when we are disturbed or unable to reach a practical solution, I suppose. Will you follow me, although I expect you know your way to the library by now? It was my late husband's greatest joy,' she added reminiscently. 'There are so many books, and he loved books almost as much as he loved music. In the end,' she added, 'he could no longer read, and I think that is where I came in. I was his eyes as well as his listening ear, and we were able to work together.'

Janet followed her with the sure feeling that they were about to become friends. She had visited the library at the *schloss* on several occasions, revelling in its wealth of literature, and sometimes she had sat down there to read instead of carrying the book she had chosen up to her bedroom. Now she felt that some of the contentment that had always reigned there still dominated the quiet room where they were about to talk, at last.

'Perhaps you should have rested after your journey from Salzburg,' she suggested.

'I have rested well enough in the car,' the Baroness told her. 'Stephen is a competent driver and I enjoy the views when we come by the back way through the mountains. I am not so fond of the autobahn, where speed has become a compulsion.'

'We came through Kitzbühel,' Janet explained, conscious of a nervousness she had not expected to feel. 'It was beautiful.'

The Baroness indicated one of the deep leather chairs beside the fire.

'Will you sit down?' she asked. 'I'm sure we have much to say to each other.'

Janet sat down on the edge of the chair, wondering how best to explain her mission.

'Richard has been searching for you for a long time,' she began, looking deeply into the older woman's eyes. 'He had traced you in Paris, but after that it was difficult. No one seemed to know where you had gone.'

'I married Stephen's father three years after I left London. There was no reason for any of my neighbours in Paris to know where I had gone. A large city is completely impersonal in some ways. James and I lived in the outskirts of Paris until he died—before Stephen was born.'

'You must have been completely shattered,' Janet sympathised.

'I was devastated. I was left on my own with a young child in a foreign country, with very little money behind me to make things a little easier, yet the only work I could do was there. I had studied in Paris and I had several contacts to fall back on, but I couldn't give my whole life over to music while Stephen was so young. I managed to get a job serving in a bakery at odd hours when someone could look after my baby, and then, when he was older, I returned to Paris. I had saved enough money to send him to a good school and I got work again in my profession, singing occasionally with an orchestra. When Stephen was old enough I managed to send him to school in England. It was what his father had wanted.'

'You never tried to contact Richard,' Janet said.

'No.' Suddenly there were tears behind the Baroness's eyes. 'How could I, with such a tale of woe to tell? We had parted in anger because we were both obsessed with our careers, with the thought of ultimate success. Love, we decided, could wait, but Richard considered it could wait in England and I had a wonderful opportunity in Paris. We were stubborn in that respect, but I wonder if we had it all to do over again if it would be different. How are we to know that sort of thing? We were young and impetuous and proud, and pride has a lot to answer for, Janet. It can so easily undermine love and slay forgiveness. Don't ever be so proud that you won't say "I'm sorry", my dear, or go back on a decision once it is made if you discover that it was a wrong decision.'

'It's difficult to see these things for oneself when you are young,' Janet said, 'but—when you have a second chance surely you can see more clearly then? Richard has never wavered in his determination to find you. All these years he has hoped to meet you again one day and—and at least talk about the past.'

The Baroness looked beyond her through the long windows where the sun was setting.

'So long ago!' she murmured. 'I would not know him now.'

'I think you would,' Janet assured her, 'because he is just the same. He hasn't changed in all the years I've known him. He brought me up, and it must have been difficult for him at times, but I never knew him as anything but kind and considerate, the sort of father I would love to have had.

He did that for fifteen vulnerable years when my life could have been so different, so I think I know him very well.'

The Baroness rose to her feet, crossing to the fireplace where the logs burned cheerfully in the wrought-iron fire-basket which was so reminiscent of Janet's first visit to the Dietrichs' shop.

'It is hard to believe,' she said after a moment, 'yet I want to believe it. Richard never married?'

'No.'

'I wonder why that was.'

'He remained in love,' Janet said. 'There was never anyone else in his life but you.'

'Yet I married happily enough,' Alice remembered wistfully. 'Stephen's father and I had much in common, but so little time together. Just enough to give me Stephen.' She turned from the fire. 'Once or twice,' she confessed, 'I was tempted to go back to London, and I did write a letter, but after I had waited and hoped for a year, there didn't seem to be much point in trying again. Pride had reared its ugly head once more and I had been offered lucrative work in Munich where I eventually met the Baron. We were friends for many years before his wife died, and they were both very good to me and to Stephen. We came here, to the *schloss*, many times for wonderful holidays which I tried to repay by working for him when his eyesight began to fail. Finally, when he was almost blind, his wife died and he was very much alone. He needed a secretary, one who realised how much his music meant to him, and finally he offered me the job. The *schloss* was so near Salzburg that I could also continue my career as a singer, although by that time I had more or less recognised my limitations. I was never going to be the famous prima donna I had set out to become, but that seemed irrelevant when I could immerse myself in music and also help someone to achieve their own life's ambition into the bargain. The Baron had composed many symphonies and had been a well known conductor for a long time, but he knew that his half-finished concerto would be his greatest work and he wanted to finish it before he was completely blind.' She walked back to the chair behind her husband's desk. 'And so,' she concluded, 'I came to the *schloss* and stayed with him till he died. We married just before then, because he wished to provide for me and for Stephen.'

She sat for several minutes in silence, reliving the traumas and the happiness of a full life until Janet asked, 'Will you agree to meet Richard now that you know the truth?'

Alice hesitated.

'I have a lot of thinking to do,' she answered slowly. 'Also, we must clear up a misunderstanding.'

'About the phone calls?'

'Yes. Stephen thought they came from London—from Richard—but I never believed that. I never thought Richard could be vindictive, and I think Stephen acknowledged the fact in the end, once he had gone into Richard's background and found out how successful he had become. Making threatening phone calls was hardly the sort of thing a barrister would do, however badly he had been hurt, so now he thinks it may be someone else, someone who may have a grudge against me for another reason.'

'I can't think that you have enemies,' Janet said impulsively. 'Who would try to frighten you like that?'

'I have no idea,' Alice said, 'but we all have enemies in one form or another, whether we realise it or not.'

Janet found herself thinking of Anastasia, but the Baroness's next remark put the idea out of her head.

'It has always been a man's voice, but it has generally been muffled,' she explained. 'I have been greatly distressed by the fact that someone wanted me to leave Austria and go back to England, although I know I shouldn't have worried so much once Stephen had reported it to the police, but sometimes when you are ill things take on greater importance. I was being asked to leave the *schloss* where I have spent so much of my time, and I could not understand why. There were even overt threats to my person if I didn't go away. "Back to where you belong" was the usual phrase, and quite often I have contemplated returning to England or even to Paris, until Stephen put a stop to any such idea. He was determined to discover who was threatening me in such a way, because it was affecting my health and he was really furious about it. He thought it was despicable that anyone should sink so low and get away with it because he can't bear injustice of any kind.'

'I don't think he would ever be unfair,' Janet responded, 'although I hardly know him. He told me some of the things you have spoken about, but there was always a reserve about him when we discussed the phone calls. I think the situation was too distressing for him to talk to a stranger about it, and I suppose I really couldn't do anything to help.'

'No.' The Baroness was looking at her thoughtfully. 'He must do this for himself, I think. My husband and he were friends,' she added slowly. 'They saw things in the same way, and Ludwig appreciated the fact that they could talk together on the same level without considering the great difference in their ages. The age-gap never really concerned them, except when Anastasia went out of her way to remind them of it. The Baron shut his sister out of his life after his marriage, I'm afraid,' she added regretfully. 'She had dominated him since childhood, the stronger personality, perhaps, but when he finally became ill he wanted only me by his side. "Anastasia is too cold, Alice," he said. "Too fond of her own way and her rights, as she calls them. Always she distresses me, always she makes me feel that I am taking too long to die." '

'How cruel!' Janet sat back in her chair. 'Perhaps the calls will cease now and let you have a measure of peace.'

'I sincerely hope so.' Alice warmed her hands at the fire, a faint colour coming into her cheeks. 'Above everything else, I don't want Stephen to sacrifice his happiness for mine. Before he goes back to Paris I must make sure of that.'

'How long does he mean to stay with you?' Janet asked.

'For a week—perhaps a little more than that if he still thinks it necessary.' The Baroness got up to stand beside Janet's chair. 'Must you go to Salzburg in the morning?' she asked. 'Your arm is not yet healed and there is no reason why you should leave.'

'I have to go,' Janet answered unhappily. 'My mission is complete. I have found you for Richard and that was why I came. Will you send for him?'

'Is that what a modern young woman would do?' the Baroness queried with a wicked smile.

'I'm sure it is!' Janet said. 'It would mean so much to him.'

'Then why don't you speak to Stephen?' Alice suggested. 'I fear he is in love with you.'

'That isn't possible,' Janet answered, although her heart had leapt at the very thought. 'Surely he is a little in love with Sophia?'

'Sophia?' Alice exclaimed. 'She is just a romantic child, far too juvenile for him and far too erratic, and no real mate for a man like Stephen. She will recover quickly and marry someone else because what she really wants is a man who will give in to her every whim, as well as one who can ski!'

'Stephen and I have never talked of love,' Janet said wistfully.

'But you will do so now when you see how foolish his mother and your guardian have been in the past?'

'Does that mean you will see Richard?' Janet rose quickly to her feet. 'You will give him a chance to make amends?'

Uncertainty still clouded the Baroness's eyes.

'We both must make amends,' she said, 'because we were equally to blame. Give me a little time, Janet, to think things over, and then I will tell you. Perhaps you need time, too,' she added. 'Go back to the Goldener Hirsch, if you must, but do not leave Austria without seeing me again.'

'I can promise you that, at least,' Janet said, aware that Alice was holding out the hand of friendship to her at last. 'Stephen has agreed to take me in the morning, but——' She hesitated. 'But I intend to phone London as soon as I get there,' she added with determination. 'I made Richard a promise and I have to keep it now that I have found you.'

The Baroness let her go, staying behind in the library with the memories the *schloss* would always hold for her until they met again over their evening meal.

For a reason of her own Anastasia decided to join them at the table, allowing Wolfgang and Gretchen, who had returned from her visit to her grandmother, to serve them. It was an uneasy meal, in spite of the effort they all made, and at the end of it Anastasia dropped her bombshell.

'As soon as I have finished packing my clothes I shall leave for London,' she announced. 'You have no need for my presence here, I'm sure, and I deserve a holiday.' She looked across the table at Sophia. 'You will come with me, of course. That is understood, since I do not think you will be welcome here, either.'

'Why have you changed your mind so suddenly?' Sophia wanted to know. 'I can ski for another week yet because the snow is still good on the high trails. Besides,' she added with a swift glance in Stephen's direction, 'who is going to take care of the Baroness?'

'That is not a problem,' her mother assured her. 'I have arranged for extra help from the village, and Gretchen and Wolfgang will be here.'

'I thought Wolf was coming to London with us as usual,' Sophia protested. 'You have always said you could not manage without him, remember?'

'That was true at one time,' Anastasia allowed, 'but now he has chosen to disobey me and he is therefore no longer in my employment. He prefers to seek his own future elsewhere.'

Stephen and the Baroness both looked astounded.

'But what will he do?' Alice asked. 'He has lived with you for years.'

'The decision is out of my hands,' her sister-in-law informed her icily, 'but I don't think you need hope to employ him. He wishes to spread his wings like all young people of his age, and therefore he must bear the consequences when things go wrong for him, as they surely will!'

True to her word, she rang for Wolfgang early the following morning, telling him to bring down her suitcases and Sophia's canvas grips, which had been hastily packed the evening before.

'I could refuse to go with her,' Sophia pointed out sullenly as she rose from the breakfast-table. 'I could easily stay here until all the snow has gone and join her later in London.'

'I think you had better go with her, Sophia,' the Baroness said. 'Your mother is no longer young and must be looked after. She needs a travelling companion and you and Wolfgang have always been there when she needed you. When you return from London, this will still be your home. I promise you that.'

Sophia heaved the deepest sigh of resignation she could produce.

'Nobody thinks about what *I* want to do,' she grumbled, 'but I suppose I shall have to go.' She looked at Stephen. 'Promise you will be in Paris when we reach there on our return!'

'I'll do my best,' Stephen answered, 'but don't take it for granted. You know how busy I am.'

'Business must be all you think about,' she accused him, 'but I mean to ask you for a job one of these days, perhaps in Paris where you have the most influence. It would be near enough to come back here to ski during the winter months.'

'Hmm,' remarked Stephen. 'We'll see.'

It was swiftly arranged that Stephen should drive them to Salzburg, where they would catch a plane for London.

'Everything is happening at the speed of sound,' Sophia remarked when, at last, they were ready to leave. 'Stephen is taking you back to the Goldener Hirsch, I understand,' she added to Janet. 'Does that mean you are returning to England?'

'In a couple of days,' Janet agreed, feeling that forty-eight hours were no time at all. By the end of it she would be saying her final goodbyes and leaving Stephen behind for ever. 'I must go back to London without too much delay.'

'Pity we couldn't travel together,' Sophia observed without a great deal of enthusiasm, 'but perhaps we shall see you in London.'

'Perhaps.'

Janet turned towards the hall where the Baroness was waiting for her to say goodbye.

'I've still got some things to collect,' Sophia said, disappearing in the direction of the cloakroom. 'Be with you in a second!'

The Baroness walked towards the library door.

'Can you spare me a minute, Janet?' she asked. 'I find it much too cold to stand in the hall, and I wish to speak to you.'

Opening the library door, she led the way in to stand beside the fire which had been newly lit.

'I have made my decision,' she said with a new determination in her eyes. 'It took me half the night, thinking this way and that, but now I am quite sure. You said you had to phone London from the Goldener Hirsch as soon as you arrived there.'

'Yes, I must contact the office,' Janet agreed, her heart beating fast as she waited for the news she hoped for. 'Richard could have returned from New York by now.'

The Baroness stood looking down into the fire for a moment or two longer.

'You must phone London for me, too,' she said, 'and I will speak to him. Yes, I have made up my mind. You must phone and I shall wait for his reaction.,'

'You know what it will be!'

The Baroness blushed.

'I'm behaving like a young girl,' she declared. 'It is, indeed, as if I had just turned nineteen again and Richard was coming to me for the first time.'

When they parted they clasped hands, meeting each other's eyes in the hope that everything would now go well for them.

They would go well for the Baroness, Janet thought, but what would she do once she had returned to London alone?

Sophia had monopolised the front passenger seat beside Stephen by the time she reached the door.

'Sit behind with Mama,' she invited. 'She will tell you all the local gossip as we go along!'

Anastasia, as usual, had little to say. Wholly occupied with her own thoughts, she sat bolt upright in the comfortable back seat, hardly offering any comment until they reached Salzburg and were driving towards the Goldener Hirsch.

'I hope you will have a pleasant journey back to England,' she said as Stephen got out to collect Janet's luggage from the boot. 'Goodbye.'

The hotel porter came from the hotel to carry her luggage in as Janet turned to Stephen, at last.

'The Baroness has agreed to see Richard,' she said. 'I hope you agree.'

'There's no reason why I shouldn't,' he answered. 'My mother usually makes her own decisions.'

'That wasn't quite what I meant.' She found explaining difficult while he continued to look at her. 'I was trying to say that I hoped you would think it was the right decision for her to make. The only one, in fact, while they could still share the rest of their lives together. They were once in love and it could be like that again, Stephen. Your mother has asked me to tell Richard when I contact him in London, and I'm quite sure he will come to meet her.'

'You will let her know,' he said, 'as soon as you can.'

She held out her hand to him.

'This must be goodbye,' she said, feeling that the whole world had turned suddenly dark. 'After I have phoned I shall return to England. Thank you,' she added. 'Thank you for all you have done.'

'We'll meet again,' he said, 'now that my mother has agreed to see Richard.'

'Some day, Stephen.' She could no longer keep the wistfulness out of her voice. 'Until then!'

'Stephen!' Sophia called from the car. 'We haven't a lot of time, and we've got to get to the airport.'

Janet bent to the window to bid Anastasia goodbye.

'Have a pleasant flight,' she said. 'You, too, Sophia. Goodbye!'

She stood waiting until the Mercedes drove away, the chill of parting numbing her mind before she turned and went in through the glass doors to the warmth of the foyer where the porter was waiting for her.

'Miss Blair?' the reception clerk acknowledged her. 'Miss Janet Blair?'

She nodded.

'Someone has been enquiring for you.' The clerk turned to take a piece of paper from a pigeon-hole in the wall behind him. 'A Mr Richard Cosgrave. He arrived early this morning and left a message for you.'

All Janet's blood seemed to rush to her head as she took the paper from him and began to read the message scrawled on it by that well-remembered hand.

> 'Have come straight from New York. Decided to join you right away. Heard you have been gallivanting elsewhere but were expected back some time today. See you! Richard.'

She could hardly believe that he was really here in Salzburg, that fate had telescoped time and they were all in one place, within touching distance—Richard and Alice and Stephen and herself—although they were not exactly paired.

'I may as well go up to my room,' she said, none too steadily. 'Will you let me know as soon as Mr Cosgrave returns?'

'Certainly, madam!'

Going up in the lift she wondered how she could possibly contact Stephen, even if it was only to let him know that Richard was in Salzburg, yet he might not want to take them back to the Schloss Erlach quite so quickly, inflicting the shock of the unexpected on his mother at such short notice, but somehow the thought of the *schloss* remained uppermost in her mind as she waited.

Just before noon Richard returned. When the telephone rang in her bedroom, she grasped it eagerly.

'Mr Cosgrave will wait for you in the foyer,' the clerk told her. 'He has just come in.'

Going down, the lift seemed to take an eternity to reach the ground floor, but at last she was there and her godfather was standing at the far side of the foyer, waiting.

'Richard!' she exclaimed, rushing towards him. 'This is the best surprise I could possibly have. One minute you're in New York, the next you're here!'

'The wonders of modern travel!' he laughed. 'I got through my business interviews sooner than I expected, and decided to come in search of you because it wasn't really fair to burden you with such a difficult task.'

'Richard, I've found her!' Janet's eyes were glowing. 'I've found Alice for you, though she isn't Alice Silton any more. She is now the Baroness Von Erlach and she is staying nearby. Up till yesterday she was here, in Salzburg, but Stephen brought her back to the *schloss.*'

'Stephen? The *schloss?* What are you talking about?' he asked, leading her to a corner table. 'Start at the beginning, if you can. Who exactly is Stephen?'

'He's—the son of her first marriage.' They settled down in the corner. 'It was all rather tragic, Richard. After she had written to you she married and had a son—Stephen—but her husband died before he was born. She has told me about the struggle she had trying to make ends meet with a young baby to look after, but she did it. Then, many years later, when Stephen graduated, she met an old friend of her husband and came to Austria as his secretary. Their mutual interest in music brought them together and she was able to help him with his work because he was going blind. When his wife died, they married.'

Told so swiftly, it seemed that the intervening years had slipped away with alarming rapidity, yet she knew how long they must have seemed for the Baroness.

Richard sat quietly in his chair, a tall, distinguished-looking Englishman considering the situation in detail before he replied.

'You said something about a letter,' he mentioned at last. 'If I had received that letter I would have gone to her, even though I had very little to offer her at the time.'

'It must have gone astray,' Janet said sympathetically. 'These things happen.'

'And alter half a lifetime.' He looked across the foyer to the crowd milling around the reception desk. 'I think you also said that she was "at the *schloss*". Is that her home these days?'

'It has been ever since her husband died,' Janet explained. 'I believe he was something of an invalid even before she married him, hardly able to see. She was his eyes, Richard, the comfort and help he needed while he finished the concerto he had worked on for many months. He needed her and, in an odd sort of a way, she needed him, too. Her career hadn't been the success she had originally hoped for, but he did help her to find other work and he was a second father to Stephen.'

'Did Stephen bring you here?' he asked.

She nodded.

'He was taking his aunt to the airport, so he brought me here on the way.'

'Does that mean you were staying at the *schloss?* And how did you get there in the first place?' he asked.

It took her a long, heavy moment to answer him.

'Stephen took me there when I thought this was far too grand and far too expensive for me.' She looked about her at their palatial surroundings. 'The Baroness has been running the *schloss* as an hotel in the mountains, with the help of her sister-in-law who has just flown out to London on holiday.'

'I can't imagine Alice as a businesswoman,' he mused. 'Not in the hotel trade, anyway. What is she like, Jan?' His eyes were eager. 'How much has she changed?'

'Not at all, I should think, speaking fundamentally, but of course I didn't know Alice Silton when you first met her.' Janet drew a deep breath. 'Now she is elegant and sophisticated—you must be prepared for that—but I think she is just the same person underneath it all.'

'Will she see me, do you think?'

'Yes.' She caught his hand. 'It's such a long story, I don't know where to begin.'

'At the beginning might be a good idea,' he suggested, as eagerly as any young lover. 'How did you trace her eventually?'

'Your clues didn't help me very much,' she told him, 'and the snapshot of Alice which was all I had to go on wasn't much better, since it was thirty years old. Also, when I reached here there seemed to be a strange conspiracy of silence when I contacted the Dietrich brothers. They didn't want to talk, and I suspect Stephen had something to do with that. The Baroness had been a good customer of theirs, and I was a stranger asking questions which they probably considered were much too personal.'

'Is that where you met Stephen?' he asked.

A slow, telltale colour stained Janet's cheeks.

'I met him in London,' she said. 'He came to the office to see you because he had traced some of your enquiries back to source. It was easy enough, I suppose, but I think he came with some sort of confrontation in mind, protecting his mother.'

'So,' he said, looking at her keenly, 'he finally brought you here?'

'It wasn't as simple as that,' said Janet. 'We met on the Orient Express and I was convinced that he was following me, which he was, in a way, because he was deeply suspicious about some phone calls the Baroness had been receiving, and I suppose he had to be sure where they were coming from.'

'Good heavens!' Richard exclaimed. 'Surely he didn't suspect me—or you, for that matter?'

'He more or less suspected everyone,' said Janet slowly. 'The Baroness had been ill, and the incessant threatening from some unknown source didn't exactly help. He was naturally very concerned, and determined to get to the bottom of the whole unsavoury affair as quickly as possible.'

'Has he done that?'

'Not yet, and I don't think he'll ever let it go. Stephen's like that.'

'Fiercely protective,' Richard mused. 'I don't wonder, when Alice did so much for him.'

'I must phone the *schloss* and tell her you are here.' Janet got quickly to her feet. 'We can't spring it on her by just arriving unannounced out of the blue. She believes she has a week or two to get used to the idea of seeing you again.'

'I'll hire a car.' He was already half-way to the reception desk. 'How far is this *schloss*, did you say?'

'I didn't, but it's quite a way into the mountains,' Janet told him. 'The roads are good, though, and most of them are clear of snow by now. You will love it, Richard! The Tyrol is such a beautiful place in early spring.'

'Yes,' he answered vaguely, not thinking about the

scenery. 'Alice must be almost fifty now.'

'Your age!' Janet smiled. 'I can't wait to see you meet!'

'I'm nervous about it, Jan,' he confessed seriously. 'She could find me changed.'

'We'll cross that particular bridge when we come to it.' Janet fumbled in her purse for some change. 'Stand by while I phone the *schloss!*'

He found the number for her in the directory.

'She may want to speak to you,' Janet warned him, and for a moment he looked oddly taken aback.

'Honestly, I won't know what to say,' he confessed.

'Which isn't your usual courtroom manner!' she teased. 'You'll know what to say when the time comes.'

She heard him sigh happily as she dialled the number.

The Baroness herself answered the telephone, a little diffidently, thinking, perhaps, of those hurtful anonymous calls which had caused her so much distress.

'The Schloss Erlach,' she announced.

'It's Jan—Janet Blair,' Janet said. 'I've got a great surprise for you.'

There was the barest pause, an indrawn breath followed by a little sigh.

'Not—Richard?' The question was eager. 'Have you been in touch with him in New York?'

'Not in New York,' Janet told her. 'Here, in Salzburg.'

'But—how could that be?' The voice was flustered. 'How could he know so quickly that I had agreed to met him?'

'He came without knowing. He flew in this morning from New York to help me with my search.'

Again a silence.

'Janet—I don't know what to say. This is all too sudden. I thought I had—a little time to come to terms with everything.'

'You know how fast things move nowadays!' Janet laughed. 'Richard is here, waiting. Will you speak to him?'

'Yes, I will!' There was resolution behind the voice now, the

Baroness she had come to know speaking with decision. 'Will you bring him to the *schloss?* I do not want to speak with him over a telephone. Perhaps I could send a hire car for you?'

'We'll arrange it,' Janet said happily. 'We can easily hire a car to bring him to you.'

'You will be sure to come?' the Baroness persisted. 'I feel that I let you go too easily. Stephen will still be at the airport, I suppose.'

'Yes.' Janet could not talk about Stephen now, although she was on her way back to the *schloss.* 'Will you have just a few words with Richard? He's here, waiting.'

She handed over the receiver, moving swiftly away to stand waiting, happily conscious of the fact that they had a great deal to say to each other. She could see Richard smiling and nodding, looking a great deal younger than he had appeared for some time. When he rejoined her, at last, he said, 'Alice thinks we should phone the airport and try to contact Stephen before we hire a car. She thinks he will want to go straight back to the *schloss.*'

'We could try,' Janet said doubtfully, 'but I don't want to—pressurise him into anything. He might even want to stay in Salzburg for a day or two.'

'We'll try, all the same.' Nothing was going to stop Richard now. 'What time does the plane go out?'

'Around midday, I think.'

Getting through to the airport took time, and more time was spent waiting for the message to be broadcast over the loudspeaker system, but after what seemed an eternity Stephen came on the line.

'It's Janet.' She could not keep the tremor out of her voice. 'I'm here at the Goldener Hirsch—with Richard.'

'Richard?' he repeated. 'How did he get there so quickly?'

'By jet from New York.' She waited for his reaction, which did not come immediately. 'Stephen, he's just been talking on the phone to the Baroness. I—I think they are very happy about the situation and—and your mother wants me to bring him to the *schloss.*' After another pause in which her heart seemed to miss a beat she added urgently, 'You do understand, don't you? He is so eager to meet her.'

'Yes, I understand,' he said, although there was still a suggestion of reserve in his voice. 'Wait where you are and I'll pick you up as soon as Anastasia's flight goes out—in another ten minutes or so.'

He rang off immediately.

'What did he say?' Richard asked.

'What could he say? He couldn't very well refuse to take us back with him when he was evidently returning to the *schloss.*'

Richard studied her keenly.

'Have you become friends?' he asked.

'Friends? Yes, I think so.'

'You sound uncertain.'

'Richard,' she said, 'I don't know what to think. I haven't known him more than a few days.'

'Sometimes it doesn't take even that long.'

'To fall in love?' she said. 'That's what you mean, isn't it?'

'To form an unalterable conviction,' he corrected.

'I've done that. Yes, I suppose I've done just that, convincing myself that I could never love anyone else. But in so short a time——'

'I don't think time really comes into it,' he said slowly. 'They were a traumatic few days, I should imagine, fraught with all sorts of doubts and misunderstandings, as far as I can gather.'

'That's true,' she agreed, turning from the telephone. 'We were rarely apart. I know he wasn't prepared to let me out of his sight because he doubted my integrity, and that was why he finally took me to the *schloss.* To keep an eye on me.'

'And now he is taking you back there.'

'Only because of you. I can't think he really wants me to go back for any other reason.'

'It will be interesting to meet him,' said Richard.

When the Mercedes drew up at the front of the hotel an hour later, they had cancelled Janet's booking and her luggage was waiting to be wheeled out ahead of them.

'I've taken so much for granted,' she said, drawing back as Stephen got out from behind the wheel. 'The Baroness didn't ask us to stay.'

'Didn't you just remark about crossing bridges when we actually came to them?' asked Richard. 'I think she will ask and, if not, we can always come back to Salzburg.'

Janet felt anxious, wondering what the two men would have to say to one another, but immediately she had introduced them she knew that they could be friends.

'I'm glad you've come,' Stephen said, looking the older man straight in the eye as they shook hands. 'It could solve a great many problems.'

'I've spoken to Alice.' Richard hadn't yet come to terms with 'the Baroness'. 'She seemed pleased.'

Stephen smiled, making no comment on the final word.

'Would you like to eat here before we go,' he asked, 'or shall we stop somewhere on the way?'

Richard glanced at his watch, the hands moving too slowly for him.

'Perhaps we could find somewhere on the way,' he suggested.

Stephen chose the tavern where Janet had waited for him at Uttendorf. It was busy when they first arrived, but a table was found for them and a quick meal provided while Richard spoke of his visit to New York. He had occupied the passenger seat next to Stephen, while Janet sat in the back listening to what they had to say, a general conversation which avoided the personal almost deliberately. Richard, impatient to meet his love of long ago, was still not sure what her son's reaction to him would be, and no doubt Stephen was still wary about accepting someone who had been a stranger to him up till an hour ago. All his preconceived opinions, even his resentments, were in the melting-pot, and she knew that he was not prepared to make a decision without giving it careful thought. Mistakes had been made in the past with hurtful results for someone he loved, and he was obstinate enough to want to be convinced, Janet decided.

They drove on, coming at last to the valley road where the *schloss* stood against the rock face on its far side, and she heard Richard draw in his breath at sight of it.

'Alice must have been happy here,' he said.

'It has been her home for the past ten years,' Stephen told him. 'She came to work here, helping with my stepfather's last concerto when he could no longer see, and that must have been fulfilment of a kind because she has always been passionately fond of music. Lately, though, I feel that she has not been happy—not entirely. She has been ill, of course, and there have been—other reasons for her not being able to settle at the *schloss*, but perhaps things will change now.'

He looked steadily ahead, as if he might see something of the future in the dark rock face as they approached, while Janet was sure that only the solution of his mother's problems would finally satisfy him.

The heavy door of the *schloss* opened as he brought the Mercedes to a standstill on the gravelled terrace above the river, and they saw the Baroness standing there, waiting.

'Alice!' Richard said as he got out. 'At last!'

She came across the terrace towards him, her hands extended in welcome, like a happy girl.

'My dear!' she said.

Janet stood back, waiting for Stephen to get out of the car.

'Surely you are pleased,' she said. 'How could you not be, seeing them together like this?' Her eyes were bright with unshed tears. 'Oh, Stephen, they have waited so long. It must be right!'

'Yes,' he said, 'I believe it is.'

Walking ahead of him into the *schloss* was like coming home, she thought, although it could only be for a little time. Gretchen was in the hall, fussing when he brought in the luggage because there was nobody there to help her.

'Where's Wolf?' he asked.

'He has gone,' Gretchen said. 'It is most sad. He was very good to work—very obedient—but he could not stay.'

'Why was that?' Stephen demanded.

'He had many words with Frau Waldburger. They did not see—how you say?—eye to eye.' She lifted Janet's suitcase. 'You have come to stay again.' She smiled. 'I am glad.'

Stephen took the case from her, lifting Richard's grip at the same time.

'I'll see to these,' he said. 'Is Miss Blair in the same room, Gretchen?'

'Yes. I prepare it for her myself when the Baroness tell me. It is most comfortable, I think.'

'I'm sure it is,' Stephen agreed, smiling at Janet for the first time. 'I'll take these up,' he said. 'Afterwards, Janet, perhaps we can talk.'

She nodded, although what he might have to say to her she could not guess, and when he came down the stairs again the Baroness was leading the way into the small dining-room.

'We're in here, Stephen!' she called. 'There are no other guests.'

Janet followed Richard into the cosy room with its tiled stove radiating a pleasant warmth and the spring sunshine slanting in at the window which looked out on the mountains. That warm sun would melt the snow, just as Richard's smile would despatch the final doubt from the Baroness's heart. Alice Von Erlach looked radiant in the simple grey dress she had chosen for this memorable occasion, with its white collar demurely encircling her throat and pinned in place with a beautiful Italian cameo, and except for the wings of white hair above each temple she could have been a girl again.

They sat at a circular table close to the stove, a foursome which could so easily have been a family party intent on exchanging news, while Gretchen served tea in the English manner.

'We dine late,' Alice explained, 'but you have had a long journey.' She looked exclusively at Richard. 'Do you survive most of the time on airport meals?' she asked.

'Not always,' he told her. 'I'm something of a culinary expert these days, as Janet will tell you. I can cook most things you care to mention, although I have been known to make the odd mistake.'

'You've no idea!' Janet laughed. 'Richard takes himself quite seriously in the kitchen, but I have had to come to his rescue on more than one occasion.'

'We're living at Beeston,' Richard explained.

'The old family home,' Alice remembered. 'I can picture you there.'

'It's rather far to travel up to London each day,' he admitted, 'but it is home for both of us. One day Janet may want to change all that,' he suggested outrageously, 'but until she marries and settles in a home of her own, she'll be more than welcome at Beeston, as she always has been.'

Janet averted her eyes because they were full of tears, and because Stephen was looking at her across the polished table.

'Richard loves Beeston,' was all she found to say.

When the meal was over they sat with their final cup of tea round the stove till the light began to fail. Alice and Richard should be alone together, Janet thought, looking at the reunited lovers.

'I fancy a breath of air,' she said, rising swiftly to her feet. 'Perhaps we could walk a little way up the valley?' She looked directly at Stephen, wondering what it was he wished to say to her. 'It's still light enough.'

He rose immediately.

'We'll leave you two to your own devices,' he said. 'You must have a lot to talk about.'

The Baroness and Richard exchanged glances.

'Only one thing,' Richard said. 'I'm going to ask Alice to come back to England with me.'

CHAPTER EIGHT

WHEN they were outside in the hall, Stephen took Janet's coat from the high-backed chair where she had left it just as the telephone bell rang in the alcove beyond.

'I wonder who that is,' he said impatiently as he went to answer it.

Slipping into her coat, Janet suddenly thought about the threatening calls which had distressed his mother so much in the past. Could this be another one, shattering the newly found peace of the old *schloss* as surely as an avalanche might have done, sweeping it to ultimate destruction so soon after it had been achieved?

She could hear Stephen's voice, sharp with command as he issued some sort of instruction, and then the dull sound of finality as he replaced the receiver on its hook. When he came out of the alcove his eyes were dark with anxiety.

'There's been an accident,' he said without preliminary. 'An avalanche has come down at the edge of the village, sweeping everything away with it. We must all help.'

'Tell me what to do,' Janet said, pushing aside the hope that had been in her heart. 'I don't suppose I'll be much use, but certainly I can do something.'

'Tell Richard,' he said, disappearing into the shadows beneath the staircase. 'We'll need lamps and ropes, and you had better borrow some stout boots from my mother. She'll know what to do.'

He had accepted her help, at least.

Richard and Alice met her at the door of the small dining-room.

'What is it?' the Baroness asked. 'I heard the telephone bell.'

'There's been an avalanche on the edge of the village,' Janet told her. 'Stephen is going out, and he thought you could get me some boots.'

The Baroness looked at Richard.

'Two pairs of boots,' he said, reaching for his coat. 'Tell Stephen I'll be with him in a minute.'

'You can't go like that,' Alice objected, her voice not quite steady. 'You'll need an anorak and some waterproof trousers, and you ought to be able to ski.'

'I could at one time,' he told her, 'and I'm told it's something that can be picked up again at a moment's notice. Where can I find the anorak?'

Janet's hands were trembling as she helped him into the borrowed jacket.

'You will be careful?'

'Certainly I will.' He looked at the Baroness. 'Just as well I came when I did!' he joked.

Stephen returned, laden with ropes and lanterns.

'These will do for a start,' he said. 'It's the usual thing as far as you're concerned,' he said to his mother. 'Sandwiches for the helpers and flasks of coffee—as many as you can muster. We could be out all night.'

Janet moved towards him. The boots the Baroness had produced for her were two sizes too big, but she wore two pairs of woollen socks with them and had stuffed her trousers into the legs. Alice's fur hat was also too big, but it would keep her ears warm.

'You look as if you were bound for the Antarctic!' Richard told her. 'You'll have to bring up the rear since you can't ski.'

'No,' she admitted, remembering her last sortie into the mountains and the stupid accident which had thrown her into Stephen's arms, 'but I can carry something,' she insisted, 'even though it is only with one hand.'

Stephen turned to look at her, noticing her for the first time as a wry smile curved his lips.

'Richard was right about the Antarctic,' he decided, 'but I think you'd better stay behind and help with the sandwiches. You can carry a basket or some kind of haversack on your good shoulder and come up with the others. Gretchen knows the way.'

Before she could protest further he had gone, taking Richard with him.

'How serious do you think it is?' she asked, cutting a long loaf into substantial sections at the kitchen table while the Baroness sliced a sausage on the chopping-board at the other end. 'Do you think there may be casualties?'

'I don't know. Sometimes these avalanches fall clear, sometimes they are disastrous, although this one may be small, since we didn't hear it coming down,' the Baroness explained.

'Can they be heard?'

'Oh, good gracious, yes!' Alice cast a quick glance towards the windows. 'When I first came here I used to think they were like wild beasts tearing down the mountainsides, and sometimes they sounded like an express train, but always they were ominous. When the snows begin to melt they are almost a daily occurrence.' She chopped the remainder of the sausage with unnecessary violence. 'I don't like them,' she decided.

'Stephen said that this one might prove quite harmless,' Janet reminded her.

'It could be.' Alice pushed a platter of yellow butter towards her. 'That doesn't mean people won't be hungry if they are forced to be out most of the night clearing up the mess.'

'I've never thought about avalanches before,' Janet confessed. 'The damage they can do——'

'They have to be thought about here and we have to live with them,' Alice returned, 'because they can come down when we least expect them. We have to be ready all the time. One minute everything can be so cosy; the next——' She left the sentence unfinished, slapping slices of red sausage between the chunks of bread. 'It's like life,' she said. 'We can't expect it to be just a rosy pathway in the sun.'

Janet parcelled up the rough sandwiches while Gretchen filled several flasks full of coffee to pack into the baskets they would carry.

'We will go quickly,' she said, 'before the light fails.'

The light was already failing as they set out, but soon a full moon had appeared above the mountain-rim in the east.

'We are fortunate,' Gretchen said. 'It will help in the rescue if there is trouble.'

Alice had stayed behind to man the telephone and heat a cauldron-like pot of soup ready for their expected return. It could all have been so different, Janet thought. Just Richard coming so unexpectedly and their love blossoming again; yet there would be other days when they could walk, hand in hand, beside the river which ran like a dark thread beside them through the snow.

'Have we far to go, Gretchen?' she asked.

'Not too long,' the village girl answered, a strong hint of anxiety in her voice now. 'Not too far.'

Suddenly there were lights ahead of them, yellow lights where the lanterns lay on the snow.

'It has come very near,' Gretchen told her. 'The village is down there.'

But something was stretched across their path, a vast river of newly disturbed snow on which dark figures were working with a kind of desperation, shovelling it aside with all their strength in an effort to reach what lay beneath.

Janet looked about her for any sign of Richard or

Stephen.

'They came up here,' she said under her breath. 'They *must* be here!'

There was hardly any talk between the men working on the snow, only the odd word of command and a pause for breath occasionally as they toiled away at the enormous broken-up surface of the avalanche. In some ways it looked almost beautiful, with a sparkle of ice on its surface and the moon shining down on it, yet beneath it lay catastrophe.

Gretchen went on ahead.

'There are four buried,' she came back to explain. 'Wolf and the friend he had in the village, and two others. They were caught in the first fall,' she added, her voice trembling.

'Wolf and his friend,' Janet repeated. 'And the other two? Did they go to Wolf's rescue?'

Gretchen nodded.

'It was very brave,' she acknowledged, 'but they also were caught. That is the way with avalanches. They are wicked things.'

Janet's lips began to tremble as she asked the question which had formed slowly in her heart.

'Who is it, Gretchen—down there?'

Gretchen eased the haversack from her shoulders, not looking at her.

'It is Herr Stephen and your friend from London,' she said.

Janet could never remember afterwards how long it took her to accept the truth. She stood there as if frozen to the spot, until the need to dispense the coffee and sustaining sandwiches prompted her into action of a kind while her heart could only echo and re-echo Gretchen's fatal words. 'Stephen and your friend from London'! Stephen and Richard buried down there under that white canopy of snow when they had attempted to rescue Wolf and his friend.

It seemed incredible, yet the men were still digging, not frantically as she had first imagined, but carefully now, anxious not to precipitate another fall of snow. The silence in which they worked seemed ominous, until she remembered that the slightest noise could so easily start another fall, buying the victims even deeper in the white shroud of the mountains.

After an hour Gretchen said that they should return to the *schloss*.

'We must prepare more coffee and tell the Baroness what has happened,' she said. 'We cannot do more to help up here while the men are still digging.'

Reluctantly Janet followed her down the way they had come, glancing back from time to time to the relentless whiteness of the mountainside, where the silent men worked out their mission of rescue in the pallid light of the moon.

The light from the *schloss* was brighter, standing out like a homing beacon above the valley to guide them, and when they reached the door the Baroness was there, waiting. She had put her grey, fur-lined cloak over her shoulders to ward off the chill of the night, and she hurried towards them with a question on her lips which had been gnawing at her heart for over two hours.

'Why have they not returned? What has happened up there to keep them so long?'

Janet clasped her hands.

'We must go inside,' she said. 'You are almost frozen, waiting here in the cold.'

Gretchen followed them in, disappearing in the direction of the kitchens to refill the flasks.

'Don't try to hide anything from me,' the Baroness said. 'What did you find up there?'

'The avalanche came down on this side of the village

and Wolfgang and a friend were caught in it.'

'Wolf?' the Baroness repeated. 'What was he doing there?'

'Visiting, I think. There was no warning when the snow came down.'

'Janet!' The Baroness took her by the shoulders. 'You must tell me the truth. It is not Wolf you want to talk about. Is it Stephen?'

Janet released her hands.

'Stephen and Richard,' she said. 'They went in to save Wolf and his friend, and then—there was another fall of snow.'

'Merciful heaven!' The older woman's face was suddenly as white as chalk. 'Are they digging now?'

'Yes. The men from the village are all there working as fast as they can. They have light from the hurricane-lamps and a full moon.'

'I must go,' the Baroness decided. 'I cannot wait here, doing nothing. We must get food and warmth to the men who are digging. That must be what Gretchen is doing in the kitchen, and we must find more flasks for her to fill.'

'Won't you wait here and let me go back with Gretchen?' Janet suggested, realising how shaken she was. 'You could get beds ready——'

'They are already prepared. When something like this happens we work to a schedule, but, Janet, it has never been like this before. I have never waited for news of the two men I love beyond anything else.'

They looked at one another, unshed tears brilliant in their eyes as they recognised their mutual anguish and their unspoken fear.

'It could end like this,' the Baroness said, 'but it must not be so, not in disaster after all these years. If Richard and Stephen come back—*when* they come back—you must tell Stephen you love him. Don't make the same mistake

Richard and I made long ago. Let him see your love. It isn't such a hard thing to do, after all.'

'If I only knew he loved me in return!' Janet said. 'But I don't. We know so little about each other. We met such a short time ago.'

'Time means very little,' the Baroness said, 'and I think I know my son.'

Gretchen came in carrying a tray with a jug and two mugs on it.

'You are cold,' she said to Janet. 'Please to drink before we go out again.'

Janet forced herself to swallow some of the hot chocolate, while the Baroness buckled on a pair of fur-lined boots.

'Are you sure you should come out?' she asked.

'Wild horses couldn't hold me back!' the Baroness said. 'I thought you understood.'

'Yes, I do,' Janet agreed, 'but please wrap up well. 'You have been ill, and it's freezing cold outside.'

'We could take the sleigh,' Gretchen suggested.

'And waste time going by the road or getting bogged down in a snowdrift?' her mistress said. 'No, Gretchen, we will travel almost as fast on our own two feet. Besides, who is here to harness the horses for us when Wolf is buried up there in the snow? We are lost without him, I have to admit.'

'Do you think he will come back?' Gretchen asked fearfully. 'He told me he was going away for always.'

'Of course he will come back!' the Baroness decided. 'Where else would he go when he did not go to London for some stupid reason of his own? Wolf has always needed direction, but he also has a stubborn streak in him which shows occasionally when he feels imposed upon or rejected,' she added thoughtfully. 'I wonder which it was this time.'

Gretchen turned away.

'He had many words with Frau Waldburger before she went to London,' she admitted slowly. 'He did not wish to go there this time and she said he must go.'

'Oh, well,' the Baroness decided, 'he had every right to refuse, and now we must hope that it has not cost him his life.'

And two other precious lives, Janet thought, walking along the stone-flagged passage to the kitchens, where an ornate urn full of mulled wine was standing near the stove, and Gretchen had already filled the flasks with fresh coffee for their return to the scene of the avalanche. She was fitting a little padded jacket round the urn, tying the tapes securely in a bow.

'That will help to keep it warm,' she said.

'People will be there from the other villages by this time,' the Baroness said, repacking the baskets, 'but food and coffee are always welcome. Can we carry the urn, do you think? It would save us coming back and forward all the time.'

'If Gretchen and I carried it, you could take a couple of baskets,' Janet suggested. 'They are not too heavy, even with the extra food.'

'We'll go along the riverbank,' the Baroness said, 'and climb up from there. What was the path like?'

'Dry and not too slippery,' Janet remembered.

'They would bring—anyone back by the path,' Gretchen said.

The Baroness paused on her way to the main door.

'Gretchen,' she said firmly, 'nobody is going to be "brought back", nobody is going to die.' Her voice had quivered on that final word, but it was the only sign of her desperate fear. 'We must be thankful that it is full moonlight and we do not have to stumble through the dark.'

When they finally began to climb, they could see the

lanterns on the hillside ahead of them, but they had still some considerable way to go. For the first time Janet became conscious of fatigue, aware of the pain in her shoulder after she had changed sides with Gretchen for the second time to lift the heavy urn up the bank.

'Put it down for a few minutes,' the Baroness advised. 'It's time we had a rest.'

Janet settled her side of the urn in the soft snowbank, but Gretchen was not so careful.

'I am glad to rest,' she acknowledged. 'My legs ache badly with those heavy boots pulling me back when I want to go forwards so much!' She sat down above the urn. 'Oh,' she exclaimed, 'now it has gone!'

Janet looked up to see the heavy urn rolling back down the slope, followed by a stream of hot, dark wine. When she looked round at the Baroness, she saw that Alice was laughing in spite of her anxiety.

'So much for the urn!' she decided. 'It will be easier to carry now that it is empty!'

'But all that wasted effort!' Janet protested. 'Should we leave it here to collect on our way back?'

'Why should we do that?' Alice returned. 'There is plenty of snow farther up, quite enough to fill several urns, and we have fuel and matches to light it with, to say nothing of the other bottles of wine we have in my baskets. The urn will boil in no time once we get there.'

Gretchen was already half-way back down the slope.

'I'll get it,' she called up to them. 'It is all very sad!'

Janet clambered down to help her, severely hampered by the roomy boots.

'They're Stephen's,' Alice told her when she reached the top of the bank once more. 'Climbing-boots. He keeps them here in the hope of coming for a holiday in the spring. I thought that was why he had come to Salzburg, but perhaps he will stay for a little while.' She bit her lip. 'Janet, if he—or Richard is injured, can you stay with me?'

She would not allow her fear to show in her eyes, but Janet recognised it in her plea for help.

'If you find you need me,' she said.

They plodded on, the urn in its padded jacket easy to carry now that it was almost empty. Up here on the snowfields it was hard and crisp underfoot, with a kneeness in the air which bit at their throats as they climbed.

'Look!' Alice said. 'Over there where all the men have gathered. They're—carrying something.'

It was a stretcher, and for a moment Janet could not bear to look.

'They're bringing someone down.' The Baroness stood arrested in her tracks. 'It's impossible to see from this distance.' She brushed a gloved hand across her eyes. 'Everyone looks alike in the moonlight, there are so many of them.'

Janet was also scanning the edge of the snowfield, but all the men walking there so purposefully could have come from the surrounding villages or scattered farms, their ski-suits practically identical in the uncertain light, the hoods laced securely under their chins.

Increasing their pace proved impossible, the deeper snow dragging at their legs as they crossed the field.

'They're coming down by the path,' Gretchen said. 'This way.'

'We'll wait.' It seemed that the Baroness had lost the power in her limbs. 'We'll wait here and cross to the path when they reach the next hollow.' She drew a quivering breath. 'Whoever it is, they're taking him back to the *schloss*.'

Stephen or Richard! Janet stood beside her in the snow, almost unable to breathe as the sharp wind cut across her face, bringing tears to her eyes. Was this to be the end of everything, of the Baroness's unexpected joy and her own longing?

The stretcher-bearers disappeared, going down on the other side of the hollow, and suddenly the Baroness was galvanised into action.

'We must be quick!' she said. 'Otherwise we shall miss them.'

Ploughing determinedly through the snow, the urn long abandoned, they came to the hard-trodden path which they had bypassed in their urgency to reach the higher slopes by crossing an open field.

'They are almost here,' Janet whispered.

The small procession advanced to be instantly recognised.

'Stephen!' Alice cried, recognising her son. 'Oh—thank God! And Richard! They are both there.'

They tried to run, still hampered by the deeper snow, until Richard saw them. Stephen was carrying one end of the stretcher. They were both safe!

'Richard,' the Baroness said as they reached the path, 'we—I thought you had been injured.'

He glanced towards the stretcher.

'It's Wolf,' he said. 'We're taking him back to the *schloss* where he was going when the avalanche struck. He is not unconscious, but he has injured his head. We've sent for a doctor.'

The Baroness clung to his hand.

'You and Stephen?' she asked. 'Are you both all right?'

'Stephen has a pretty nasty graze on the side of his face, but I dare say he'll live!' He smiled for her benefit, turning to Janet at last. 'What about you, Jan? Are you all right? You look as if you've seen a ghost.'

'A—very active ghost!' She was looking at Stephen walking past with the stretcher, a world of love in his eyes. 'I can't tell you how—glad I am.'

A poor word, she thought. Glad, when her heart was

suddenly overflowing with happiness, an inadequate thing, but all her relief and thankfulness had been expressed in those last three words.

The doctor had reached the *schloss* by the time they got there, his car parked on the frost-hardened gravel before the main door.

'I hope he's had the sense to go in,' Alice said. 'The door was open.'

An enormous, bearded man in baggy *Lederhosen* came towards them as they entered the hall.

'Dr Pacher!' the Baroness greeted him. 'You are here before us!'

The doctor's eyes were on the stretcher which Stephen was guiding in through the doorway.

'Is he still concussed?' he asked, moving to his patient's side. 'Ah, I see it is Wolfgang! What is he trying to say?'

'Something about having to speak to me,' Stephen answered, 'but that can wait till you patch him up.'

'The graze on your own forehead,' the doctor mentioned. 'Have you the dizziness—or perhaps a headache?'

Stephen dismissed the idea.

'Nothing like that,' he said. 'Let's see to Wolf.'

As he passed her, Janet put out her hand to touch his sleeve.

'Are you sure, Stephen?' she asked. 'It's important.'

He looked at her in the yellow glow of lamplight with something in his expression which stirred a wild hope in her heart.

'We must see to Wolf,' he said. 'Richard and I have escaped with no more than a bruise or two, so stop worrying about us!'

'How could we help worrying?' she said. 'It seemed as if you—had both gone.'

He went in with the stretcher, helping to settle Wolf by the fire while the doctor made a swift examination to assess the damage he had suffered.

'It is little,' he announced at last. 'A slight head wound which I can now stitch, and a wrenched muscle or two. He has been very lucky,' he decided, turning to the Baroness, who had greeted him as an old friend. 'You will have to keep him in bed till tomorrow,' he decided. 'There is some shock, also, but he is young and will soon recover.'

'I'll see to it,' Alice promised, 'and you will stay and take a meal with us, Dr Pacher.'

'Alas!' he said, shaking his head. 'I must refuse, much against my will, you understand? I have a patient in the village about to give birth to her first child, and I must be there because I fear a difficult delivery. You will excuse me, I'm sure.'

The Baroness nodded. Gretchen had brought hot water and a supply of clean white towels which he accepted with a twinkle in his eye.

'I am not about to cut his head off, Gretchen,' he said. 'One towel will do!'

Carefully he stitched the gash in Wolf's head, inserting the stitches neatly and stepping back at last to admire his handiwork.

'There you are!' he said to Anastasia's henchman. 'You are now as good as new. But why, I ask, are you not in London? I have been told that Frau Waldburger left early this morning.'

'I did not go with her. I did not want to go to London again.' Wolf's gaze travelled swiftly to Stephen. 'I have to speak to you,' he repeated.

'All in good time.' Stephen followed the other members of the stretcher party across the hall. 'You will take some refreshment,' he offered.

The Baroness went with the three men to the kitchens, with Gretchen hurrying behind because one of the stretcher-bearers was her brother. Stephen sat down by the fire when the doctor had gone.

'Now you can talk, Wolf,' he said. 'What is it you wish to say to me?'

'It is about Frau Waldburger.' Wolf's expression was grim. 'It has taken me a long time not to obey her any more, but now I have decided to be free. I will no longer do her bidding and hurt the Baroness into the bargain. You see—I made the telephone calls which so distressed her, and for that I am ashamed. I do not expect your forgiveness. I do not expect to remain here when I am well enough to go. You have saved my life and the life of my friend, Graf, and all I have done is to betray you, but I could not refuse her when she had employed me for so long.' He drew a deep breath, still looking earnestly at Stephen. 'Frau Waldburger was determined to be rid of the Baroness in one way or another, and she thought that fear would make her leave the *schloss* one day. Frau Waldburger believed that she could frighten her away, making her feel unwanted and full of guilt at inheriting everything from the Baron.' He drew another deep, quivering breath. 'It was against my principles,' he confessed, 'but I was hard-pressed. If I had no references, how could I find another job?'

Janet moved away from the fireplace where the flickering yellow flame lit up all the anger in Stephen's face. He would never forgive Wolf, she thought, for what he had done to his mother, even though he had been acting by proxy for Anastasia, whose jealousy knew no bounds, yet when she thought more deeply about Wolf's confession she was conscious of an overwhelming relief. The conversation she had just overheard cleared away much of the doubt and suspicion which had existed between them, and perhaps they could now be friends.

She looked about her for the others, but the hall was empty. Richard and Alice had gone to the study, while Gretchen had returned to the kitchens to prepare a meal for the stretcher party. There seemed nowhere for her to go. Looking back towards the fire, she saw Stephen bending over Wolf as if to reassure him, and she could not interrupt what had been, after all, a confession of guilt on Wolf's part.

Turning to the door, she went out again into the cold night, walking quickly along the length of the terrace to keep warm.

It was some minutes before the doctor drove away, and another ten before Gretchen ushered her brother and his companions out into the night. Janet watched as they hurried away, warmed by the food and drink as they bore the stretcher back to the village to drink schnapps or brandy, as the spirit moved them, far into the night while they discussed the adventure which had befallen them without causing too much trouble in the end.

When Stephen came to look for her she was still standing at the terrace edge, and suddenly she felt his hands on her shoulders, turning her to face him in the silver light.

'I misjudged you, Jan, right from the beginning,' he said, 'so how can you ever forgive me? I love you—I must tell you that—but you have every right to reject me.'

'Reject you?' She looked up at him, echoing his words as if she could hardly believe them. 'Oh, Stephen,' she said, 'how could I ever do that? No matter what you have done, I could not send you away.' She reached up to kiss his cheek. 'Never!'

Instantly she was in his arms, crushed against him with the bitter cold of the night shut out and the warmth of his strong, taut body her immediate comfort.

'I love you,' he said, his lips close against her own. 'I shall always love you, Jan.' Again he kissed her, strong and demandingly. 'Tell me you will stay here till we have time to plan our future together. Tell me you have no intention of going away!'

'I could say that so easily and so easily mean it,' she confessed, clinging to his wet anorak, 'but I may have to return to London and you to Paris. At this moment I want to pretend that the whole world doesn't matter, though. Only the two of us.'

He silenced her effectively with another kiss.

'We won't be parted,' he said. 'I'm coming back to London with you on your godfather's invitation, and we will discuss all this at Beeston. I had made up my mind to ask you to marry me in your old home,' he added, still holding her close, 'but tonight has made a difference. Tell me that you agree!'

'I—thought I had lost you,' she said unsteadily. 'When you went out with Richard to find Wolf, the Baroness—your mother and I wondered if we would ever see you again—alive. She knew about the avalanches, Stephen, and I think she feared the worst, although she wouldn't admit it. To me,' she added slowly, 'it seemed that fate might deal her the cruellest blow of all, losing you both when she had only just found Richard again.'

He looked back towards the *schloss* where the lights were shining out as if in welcome.

'We'll give them another minute or two before we go in,' he suggested, leading her away from the terrace edge with a protective arm about her shoulders. 'They deserve it after so long a time. They're going to be happy together—you can see it just by looking at them, so you needn't regret your journey on the Orient Express!'

'I never shall,' she said, turning her head to kiss the back of his supporting hand. 'It was the happiest journey I have ever made.'

'Even although you suspected me of following you?' he teased lightly.

She smiled.

'At first I couldn't make up my mind,' she said, 'but now

I'm glad you did!'

'I should never have doubted you,' he returned more seriously, 'but some of those calls Wolf has now admitted to came from London, and there was also the fact that someone was trying to trace my mother's movements since Paris, and I was determined to find out who it was to save her further heartache. I thought the calls and the investigation were connected, you see, and so I have misjudged Richard, too. I'm sorry about that,' he acknowledged, 'because I think we have now become friends.'

'Will the Baroness come to London?' Janet asked.

'I think it is something she has always wanted. It will be going home as far as she's concerned.'

'What about the *schloss?*'

'My mother will keep Wolf in her service, in spite of everything,' he said, 'and if Anastasia wants to come back here and run the hotel, she will be welcome to do that, too. The Baroness Von Erlach has a forgiving nature!'

'And you, Stephen?' Janet asked, holding on to his hand. 'Can you ever forgive me for coming here more or less under false pretences?'

'I was coming to that,' he said, leading her towards the main door. 'I don't think I ever really doubted you after our first encounter on the train, but I have a stubborn streak in me that makes me want to be sure.'

'Are you sure now? Absolutely sure?' she asked.

His arm tightened around her.

'You must tell me that,' he said. 'You have proved so many things to me, such as love never doubting and being constantly kind.'

'Don't put a halo round my head!' she laughed.

'I won't,' he promised. 'I want you down to earth, here in my arms!'

Richard and Alice met them in the hall, warm and

glowing with love.

'Nearly thirty years!' Alice said softly. 'It's a very long time to wait for an ordinary phone call, and I could have waited for the rest of my life if it hadn't been for Richard's determination to find me.'

Stephen took Janet's hand.

'We're not making the same mistake,' he said firmly. 'I'm keeping you under surveillance now till you marry me!'

INDULGE A LITTLE SWEEPSTAKES

OFFICIAL RULES

SWEEPSTAKES RULES AND REGULATIONS. NO PURCHASE NECESSARY.

1. NO PURCHASE NECESSARY. To enter complete the official entry form and return with the invoice in the envelope provided. Or you may enter by printing your name, complete address and your daytime phone number on a 3 x 5 piece of paper. Include with your entry the hand printed words "Indulge A Little Sweepstakes." Mail your entry to: Indulge A Little Sweepstakes, P.O. Box 1397, Buffalo, NY 14269-1397. No mechanically reproduced entries accepted. Not responsible for late, lost, misdirected mail, or printing errors.

2. Three winners, one per month (Sept. 30, 1989, October 31, 1989 and November 30, 1989), will be selected in random drawings. All entries received prior to the drawing date will be eligible for that month's prize. This sweepstakes is under the supervision of MARDEN-KANE, INC. an independent judging organization whose decisions are final and binding. Winners will be notified by telephone and may be required to execute an affidavit of eligibility and release which must be returned within 14 days, or an alternate winner will be selected.

3. Prizes: 1st Grand Prize (1) a trip for two to Disneyworld in Orlando, Florida. Trip includes round trip air transportation, hotel accommodations for seven days and six nights, plus up to $700 expense money (ARV $3,500). 2nd Grand Prize (1) a seven-night Chandris Caribbean Cruise for two includes transportation from nearest major airport, accommodations, meals plus up to $1,000 in expense money (ARV $4,300). 3rd Grand Prize (1) a ten-day Hawaiian holiday for two includes round trip air transportation for two, hotel accommodations, sightseeing, plus up to $1,200 in spending money (ARV $7,700). All trips subject to availability and must be taken as outlined on the entry form.

4. Sweepstakes open to residents of the U.S. and Canada 18 years or older except employees and the families of Torstar Corp., its affiliates, subsidiaries and Marden-Kane, Inc. and all other agencies and persons connected with conducting this sweepstakes. All Federal, State and local laws and regulations apply. Void wherever prohibited or restricted by law. Taxes, if any are the sole responsibility of the prize winners. Canadian winners will be required to answer a skill testing question. Winners consent to the use of their name, photograph and/or likeness for publicity purposes without additional compensation.

5. For a list of prize winners, send a stamped, self-addressed envelope to Indulge A Little Sweepstakes Winners, P.O. Box 701, Sayreville, NJ 08871.

DL-SWPS

INDULGE A LITTLE SWEEPSTAKES

OFFICIAL RULES

SWEEPSTAKES RULES AND REGULATIONS. NO PURCHASE NECESSARY.

1. NO PURCHASE NECESSARY. To enter complete the official entry form and return with the invoice in the envelope provided. Or you may enter by printing your name, complete address and your daytime phone number on a 3 x 5 piece of paper. Include with your entry the hand printed words "Indulge A Little Sweepstakes." Mail your entry to: Indulge A Little Sweepstakes, P.O. Box 1397, Buffalo, NY 14269-1397. No mechanically reproduced entries accepted. Not responsible for late, lost, misdirected mail, or printing errors.

2. Three winners, one per month (Sept. 30, 1989, October 31, 1989 and November 30, 1989), will be selected in random drawings. All entries received prior to the drawing date will be eligible for that month's prize. This sweepstakes is under the supervision of MARDEN-KANE, INC. an independent judging organization whose decisions are final and binding. Winners will be notified by telephone and may be required to execute an affidavit of eligibility and release which must be returned within 14 days, or an alternate winner will be selected.

3. Prizes: 1st Grand Prize (1) a trip for two to Disneyworld in Orlando, Florida. Trip includes round trip air transportation, hotel accommodations for seven days and six nights, plus up to $700 expense money (ARV $3,500). 2nd Grand Prize (1) a seven-night Chandris Caribbean Cruise for two includes transportation from nearest major airport, accommodations, meals plus up to $1,000 in expense money (ARV $4,300). 3rd Grand Prize (1) a ten-day Hawaiian holiday for two includes round trip air transportation for two, hotel accommodations, sightseeing, plus up to $1,200 in spending money (ARV $7,700). All trips subject to availability and must be taken as outlined on the entry form.

4. Sweepstakes open to residents of the U.S. and Canada 18 years or older except employees and the families of Torstar Corp., its affiliates, subsidiaries and Marden-Kane, Inc. and all other agencies and persons connected with conducting this sweepstakes. All Federal, State and local laws and regulations apply. Void wherever prohibited or restricted by law. Taxes, if any are the sole responsibility of the prize winners. Canadian winners will be required to answer a skill testing question. Winners consent to the use of their name, photograph and/or likeness for publicity purposes without additional compensation.

5. For a list of prize winners, send a stamped, self-addressed envelope to Indulge A Little Sweepstakes Winners, P.O. Box 701, Sayreville, NJ 08871.

© 1989 HARLEQUIN ENTERPRISES LTD.

DL-SWPS

INDULGE A LITTLE—WIN A LOT!

Summer of '89 Subscribers-Only Sweepstakes

OFFICIAL ENTRY FORM

This entry must be received by: Sept. 30, 1989
This month's winner will be notified by: October 7, 1989
Trip must be taken between: Nov. 7, 1989–Nov. 7, 1990

YES, I want to win the Walt Disney World® vacation for two! I understand the prize includes round-trip airfare, first-class hotel, and a daily allowance as revealed on the "Wallet" scratch-off card.

Name________________________________

Address______________________________

City__________ State/Prov.______ Zip/Postal Code______

Daytime phone number____________________
Area code

Return entries with invoice in envelope provided. Each book in this shipment has two entry coupons — and the more coupons you enter, the better your chances of winning!

© 1989 HARLEQUIN ENTERPRISES LTD.

DINDL-1